The Kingfisher let out a high-pitched scream that would have done a woman justice. Then the tall, tan-complexioned man began to scramble toward the waiting car. He had to shove some of his bodyguards out of the way, but he managed to throw himself through the front door of the waiting Cadillac before the Ford reached them. Some of his gunmen, made out of better stuff, held their ground, pulling guns from under their coats. But the pistols were no match for the bursts from the submachine guns as the car roared past. All the bullets that struck the Cadillac bounced off because the car was bulletproof. But the men standing on the sidewalks weren't. They fell as if someone had cut them down with a mowing machine!

DEATH LIST

DONALD GOINES

Kensington Publishing Corp.
http://www.kensingtonbooks.com

HOLLOWAY HOUSE CLASSICS are published by

Kensington Publishing Corp.
119 West 40th Street
New York, NY 10018

All Kensington Titles, Imprints, and Distributed Lines are
available as special quantity discounts for bulk purchases
for sales promotions, premiums, fund-raising, and educa-
tional or institutional use. Special book excerpts or cus-
tomized printings can also be created to fit specific
needs. For details, write or phone the office of the Kensington special sales manager: Kensington Publishing
Corp., 119 West 40th Street, New York, NY 10018, attn:
Special Sales Department, Phone: 1-800-221-2647.

Holloway House Reg. U.S. Pat. & TM Off.

ISBN-13: 978-0-7582-8648-2
ISBN-10: 0-7582-8648-1

First Kensington trade paperback printing: March 2013

10 9 8 7 6 5 4 3 2 1

Printed in the United States of America

DEATH
LIST

1
___

THE TWO DETECTIVES had been sitting in their office at the downtown police precinct since early morning, waiting for one phone call. When the telephone finally rang, both men leaped to their feet. The black officer beat his white partner to the phone. He winked at his friend, letting him know that this was the call they had been waiting for.

The tall, chisel-faced white man walked back to his old beat-up desk and sat down. Detective Ryan drummed his fingers on the top of the well-scarred desk as he waited impatiently for the call to come to an end.

Finally the tall black man hung up the phone. "Well, what the hell are you going to do," he yelled over to his partner as Ryan jumped to his feet, "sit there on your dead ass all day?"

"Screw you, Benson, you cocksucker you," Ryan yelled back as both men moved hurriedly towards the door. "Did the informer give up all the information we need?"

Detective Edward Benson slowed down enough to show Ryan a piece of paper on which he had hurriedly written down an address. "We've got the bastard's address, just like he said he'd get."

The two men walked hurriedly down a short corridor that led into an outer office. The detectives threaded their way through the cluttered office, greeting the men and women over the hum of the old-fashioned air conditioner.

As the black and white detectives neared the outer door, two younger detectives sitting nearby came to their feet. Neither man appeared to be over twenty-five years old, while Benson and Ryan both had wrinkles under their eyes that were not there from lack of sleep. Both of the older detectives appeared to be in their late thirties or early forties. They were replicas of what the younger men would look like in ten years if they stayed on their jobs as crime fighters. The work would take its toll.

The two young white detectives ignored Benson and spoke to his partner. It was done more out of habit than to slight Benson deliberately. "We were told to wait for you, sir, that you might need backup men," the taller of the two said.

Ryan stopped and stared at the men. He hadn't missed the slur to his black partner. "I don't know," Ryan answered harshly. "It's up to my senior officer, Detective Benson." He nodded in the direction of the black officer.

The two young white detectives glanced down at the floor in embarrassment. Neither man wanted to come out and ask Benson directly if they could go along, but it would be a good point on their record if they could be in on the arrest of two murderers.

"What do you think, Ben?" Ryan asked his partner, breaking the silence.

Benson glanced coldly at the two younger officers. "It's up to you, Ryan, if you think you might need some help arresting the punks." He shrugged his shoulders, showing by his actions that he really didn't want the men along.

Ryan knew what the problem was. If the men had spoken to Benson when they first walked up, he would have taken them along gladly. But now he didn't want to be bothered with them. It was written all over his face. In the years Ryan had worked with him, he had come to find that the intelligent black man was extremely sensitive. At times, it seemed as if he was too sensitive. Ryan started to tell the young men to come along anyway but changed his mind. There was no sense in antagonizing the man he had to work with.

As Benson went out the door, Ryan turned to the two men sheepishly. "Well, I guess there won't be any need for your help after all. It shouldn't take four of us to bring in two punks."

It was apparent that the two men were disappointed. One of them started to say something but decided against it. Their brief exchange hadn't gone unnoticed by some of the other officers in the department. Most of them had been aware of what the men had been waiting for. As Ryan went out the door, leaving the men behind, the workers in the office glanced down, not wanting to catch the eyes of the rejected men.

Ryan caught up with his partner in the garage underneath the station. This was where they brought their prisoners. They took them out of the cars, still handcuffed, and led them to the three elevators that were located in the center of the garage. No matter where a policeman parked, he didn't have far to go to transport his prisoner. There were two uniformed policemen stationed in the garage at all times to help, if help was ever needed. The garage was also a good place for the policemen to kick the shit out of their prisoners, out of sight of any watching eyes. The garage detail never went against another officer, no matter how brutally policeman might treat a handcuffed prisoner.

"You could have brought those guys along, Ryan," Benson said, drumming his fingers impatiently on the steering wheel.

Ryan shook his head as Benson drove out of the garage. "Naw, Ben, it's like you said; what the hell do we need with help? It ain't but two punks that we're after."

Benson knew Ryan was lying, as well as he knew

he had been wrong in rejecting the help of the fellow officers. They were on their way to arrest Billy Good and his crime partner, Jackie Walker. Both men were believed to be professional killers. In such a case, there should be backup men on the job. If something should happen to Ryan because of Benson's anger, he would never get over it. But as he picked up the two-way radio and put in a call, giving the address they were headed for and requesting the support of a black-and-white car, Benson got a feeling of satisfaction. He knew that the two younger detectives would hear about it and know they had been rejected while two uniformed men had been called in to do what they had been refused the honor of doing.

Ryan only glanced straight ahead. He knew what his partner had done and realized that it was another blow to the pride of the younger officers. As it was, Benson wasn't the most liked officer in the homicide division. And after this got out, which it would, he would be liked even less.

"You think these guys will give us any trouble?" Ryan asked as they left the freeway at Clay Avenue and made a left turn.

Benson gave his standard shrug. "I haven't thought about it one way or the other. I could care less either way," he answered coldly.

Even as the policemen got off the freeway eight blocks from their destination, events were taking place that would change their lives.

Billy Good was parking the car in front of his

and Jackie's apartment. Jackie kissed his girl-friend, Carol, one more time before getting out. They had just come from Kenyatta's farm, where they had been staying for the past week. Ever since making the hit on Kingfisher's dope pusher, Little David, they'd been out of town.

Billy, who had driven the whole way back from the farm, stretched his arms out, then caressed Joy's neck. The tall, black beauty riding next to him smiled contentedly. Joy had finally found a man she could really love. This short, husky, brown-skinned man wasn't what she'd dreamed her lover man would look like, but he'd proven he was more than adequate. She had no apprehensions when she was with him, It was a new and gratifying experience for her.

The men she'd had in the past had always depended on her, mostly for an income. Now she had a man who wasn't concerned with how much money she could make. He just wanted her for herself.

This was the first time Joy had ever been to the apartment that Billy shared with Jackie. She had just met Billy when Kenyatta brought him and Jackie out to the farm and had given a party in their honor. She smiled to herself smugly as she remembered that first night in Billy's arms. What a night it had been! They'd made love until dawn, and then she couldn't really sleep, afraid that when she awoke it would all have been a dream.

Carol and Jackie got out of the car first and

waited on the pavement for Billy to come around the car and join them. They made a curious couple, him being over six foot five while she was only five foot.

Billy came around the car grinning. Neither of the two couples paid much attention to the well-dressed black men who got out of the black Cadillac down the street and hurried toward them. The first warning came when the men had gotten close and Jackie noticed one of them open up his suitcoat and take out what looked like a short iron pipe. Before he could react, he realized that it was a sawed-off shotgun.

He screamed out in panic. "Watch out, Billy, they got shotguns!"

The sound of his voice hadn't died out before the afternoon quiet was shattered by the sound of shotguns going off.

Joy had been admiring the new home she was going to move into when she was struck down. Half of her neck was blown off. Billy was spattered with the blood of his loved one. He screamed—a dying scream full of hate and frustration as he made a frantic move for his shoulder holster. Unknown strength kept him on his feet as the first shotgun shells hit him high in the chest. He fell back against the car, somehow managing to remove the gun from its place of concealment. But it was no use. He died with the weapon still in his hand.

Carol's screams shattered the stillness as she

watched Jackie topple over, his tall frame crumbling as he kept falling until the hard pavement struck him in the face. Her screams were cut off abruptly as half her mouth and face were blown away. She was dead before she hit the cold ground.

Black faces peered out of the windows of the nearby buildings, but no one came to the rescue of the stricken couples. Blood ran freely down off the sidewalk into the gutter as the lifeless forms of four young black people lay in the filth and hopelessness of the hard-pressed neighborhood.

Down the street, the long black Cadillac moved away from the curb, filled with black men who made killing their business. Even as Detectives Benson and Ryan turned onto the street, the black car disappeared around the corner.

Benson slammed on his brakes next to the murder scene. The black-and-white backup car came from the opposite end of the street, having turned the same corner that the black Cadillac had.

Benson walked from one body to the next, examining the dead. When he reached Jackie's long body, he thought he heard a moan, but there was so much blood he believed it must be his imagination. He bent down and lifted up the bloody head, cradling Jackie in his arms as if he were a loved one.

"I think this one is still with us," he yelled out as Ryan came over.

Ryan flinched at the sight. He had seen many murders before, but whenever he came upon a shotgun killing, it was always horrible. This one was even worse than most. It was the first time he'd ever seen women shot down in such a vicious manner.

Ryan stood over his partner and called out to one of the uniformed officers who was running over with a gun in his hand. "Call for an ambulance," he ordered sharply, his voice cracking with emotion.

As Ryan glanced around at the other uniformed policeman, he saw the young black officer bent over by the car, throwing up his afternoon meal. The sight of the man puking almost made Ryan do the same thing.

Benson stood up. "He can change that call; we don't need an ambulance. What we need is a meat wagon." He walked away, unaware of the blood that was on his new blue suit.

2

THE PRIVATE OFFICE in the rear of Kenyatta's club was crowded with members. Ali had brought most of the main people in from the farm, and they were all trying to get in the rear office. The front of the club was full of the less important members of the organization. All of the talk floating around was about the killing of Billy and Joy, with little mention of Jackie and Carol. Joy and Billy were the better known of the four people. As they talked about the killings, the young people in the crowd couldn't really believe what had happened, or didn't want to.

The men spoke in loud voices about retaliation and the punishment that Kenyatta would dish out for the wrong done them. Even though Billy and Jackie hadn't been members, their women had been members. And Joy was related to Kenyatta's lady, Betty, so they knew something would be done.

12   Even as they whispered about it, Kenyatta paced up and down his office. "It has to he an act of retaliation, Ali," Kenyatta stated, stopping in front of the tall, baldheaded man. "No matter how I look at this shit, it comes up the same way. That motherfucking nigger Kingfisher is behind this crap. I'll bet my front seat in hell, man, that he put out the contract on Billy and them because of that pusher Little David gettin' hit."

Betty got up from the hardbacked wooden chair she had been sitting in at the rear of the office. The stately, beautiful woman walked up to her man and stopped. "But why, honey, why did they kill Joy? She didn't have anything to do with the killing of Little David. She wasn't even in the city at the time." Tears were running down her cheeks as she talked. "I can't get it out of my mind that it was my fault that Joy got killed."

"Hold on, baby," Kenyatta said softly, taking the girl's arm and drawing her near. He held her tight in his arms and stroked her hair tenderly. "Get them kind of thoughts out of your mind," he said as he gently led her toward his large chair behind the desk.

"It's true, though, Ken," she continued. "If I hadn't introduced her to Billy, it would never have happened. She wouldn't have been with him when he came back to town, so she wouldn't have gotten killed."

"Honey," Kenyatta whispered, "you can't think like that. The way them two fell in love with each other, it couldn't have went any other way. I mean, they would have met anyway. He stayed out on the farm after we left, so they would have come in contact with each other no matter what you did." Before she could speak, he continued. "Lookin' at it that-away, Betty, you can hold me responsible for their deaths, because if I hadn't given the party for them, none of this would have jumped off."

Betty stared up at the tall black man she loved. She gained strength from him, and at that moment she needed all the strength she could get. His words took her doubts and fears away.

She allowed him to sit her down in his chair. "When you talk, honey, it all makes sense, but when I get to thinkin' by myself, I keep seeing myself as the reason why she's dead."

"Well, don't think then," Kenyatta stated, ignoring the rest of the people in the office. He was tired of the crowd of people anyway, but he didn't want to dismiss them. He was going to need some of them as soon as some information came in, so he'd just have to put up with the crowd for a while.

"He's sure tellin' you right, momma," Ali said as he reached over on the desk and picked up one of Kenyatta's cigarettes. "The way them two carried on, it was just in the cards, that's all."

She glanced at the two men. They were so

much alike, not just for the fact that they both were baldheaded, either. Both were tall black men, but whereas Kenyatta wore a beard and heavy mustache, Ali wore only a trimmed mustache. Ali was slightly taller than Kenyatta, too, though both men towered over six feet.

Kenyatta raised his hands for quiet, then spoke to the group in his office. "Fellows, you and the few ladies in here, I want you people to go upstairs or into the outer office until Ali and I can get something together. It's not that I ain't got faith in all you brothers and sisters, nor am I holding any secrets from you, but it's just that there's too many people in here now. We can't even hear ourselves think, so you go upstairs and have fun. I'll call the ones I want."

He waited until most of the people filed out the door. Betty started to leave, but Kenyatta waved her back down in her chair. "I'll tell you what you can do, Betty. Fix me and Ali a good cold drink, okay? Then come on back down."

She smiled at him as she got up to do as he requested.

Both men watched the tall, attractive black woman as she walked across the office floor. The thick, dark brown carpet smothered the sound of her high-heeled shoes, but nothing could disguise her large, beautiful black thighs, revealed to the eye by the miniskirt she wore. The tiny red skirt bounced up behind her with each step she took, causing Ali to give her a long admiring glance.

Both men remained silent until the door closed behind Betty. She was the last person to leave the office.

Ali let out a short whistle. "I got to admit she sure is a looker."

It seemed as if Kenyatta hadn't even heard his remark. The dark, handsome man walked to the rear of the office and stared out the window. He didn't bother to speak for a few minutes. "Ali, it's like I said. Ain't but one person responsible for this mess, and that's that nigger Kingfisher. I want him. I want him so bad I can taste it. That nigger is to blame for over half the dope that comes into the ghetto, Ali. Over half the fuckin' poison that finds its way into those dumb-ass addicts' veins."

Ali was used to his partner's ways, so he just remained silent and waited. "We," Kenyatta began softly, "were supposed to have knocked off that food stamp place. That's what Billy came back to town for. I called him and told him to get his ass on back here if he wanted in on the stickup." He stopped as if deep in thought, then added, "Then them niggers shot him down. He must have just pulled up in front of their apartment when them motherfuckers cut them down."

There were actually tears in Kenyatta's eyes as he talked. Ali glanced away so that Kenyatta wouldn't realize that he had seen them. Ali knew that the killing of their friends had hit Kenyatta hard, but he hadn't figured it had hit him that hard. Actually, Ali could take it in stride. So a couple of gunmen and their broads had got knocked off. Those things happened when you played in the big leagues.

"I got a call, Ali," Kenyatta began, changing the subject, "from my white boy who's gettin' that list for us. He's got it. Now all we need is the cash I promised him for it."

That was something else Ali didn't agree with. Paying out all that money for a list of dope dealers just didn't make sense, even if they were the largest dealers in the city. The thought of ten thousand dollars going out for a piece of paper with names on it was just too much for Ali to understand. He wished at times that he was the leader. Then he'd run the organization differently. While it was a good idea preaching about knocking off the dope pushers, it would pay even better if they just made the pushers pay them protection. But Kenyatta wouldn't hear of anything like that. He was really sincere when he preached that shit about cleaning up the ghettos. If he wasn't, he wouldn't be wasting time killing police who came down on the brothers. Any time they got a report about any nigger-hating cop, Kenyatta started planning on sending the cop to hell.

"You still plannin' on payin' that 'wood all that money for that list, Kenyatta?"

"Uh huh, ain't nothin' changed. Why should it?" Kenyatta turned away from the window. "You ain't never been able to accept the idea of puttin' out all that bread for them names, have you?" He waited, then continued before Ali could answer. "I don't see why it's so hard for you to understand. Ali, the first time we knock off a pusher, we ought to be able to pick up more cash than I'm settin' out for the list. Man, all these mothers on the list are big, and do I mean big. They are the bastards that supply the dope to the whole damn city, Ali. They ain't just neighborhood pushers, man. They're what you would call international dope men. Just about every name on the list will be a whitey, baby, so you can imagine the kind of dough they should have around their pads."

For a minute the men's eyes met in a clash of wills. Finally Ali had to glance down at the rug. There was something fanatical in Kenyatta's eyes. It occurred to him that the man was mad.

"Yeah, man, what you say sounds good," Ali began, "but it might just be a little more difficult than what you think. Them honkies have got guards all over the fuckin' place. If they were easy to knock off, somebody would have knocked them off before now."

"That's the goddamn problem with black men," Kenyatta stated coldly. "You big-ass bad brothers are always ready to step in and knock off another black man who's dealing, but when it comes to steppin' on them peckerwoods' toes, you start shittin' in your pants." Kenyatta walked over to Ali and looked straight into his eyes. "I know damn near what you think before you think it, Ali, and don't you ever forget it. I know you'd just love to be number one in this outfit, but it wouldn't work. They wouldn't follow you for ten minutes. You think small and you'll always be small." Kenyatta raised his voice. "If you think I'm lying just look in the mirror. When I mentioned knockin' off them rich honkies, your face damn near turned red, and that's one hell of a trick for a black-ass nigger like you!"

For the second time in less than ten minutes Ali found himself unable to look into Kenyatta's eyes. This time it was for a different reason. He stared down at the rug, ashamed of what he felt.

"It ain't like that at all, Kenyatta. I'm just lookin' at facts, man. Them honkies you're talkin' about ain't goin' be easy to reach. They don't even allow a black face out in them neighborhoods. That's why I say we don't stand a chance of knockin' them 'woods off."

"Niggers walk into banks and knock them off every motherfuckin' day, Ali, so why should it be too difficult for a black man to figure out a way to knock off some goddamn peckerwood just because he lives in a neighborhood that don't want any black people moving in? We got a few light-skinned black people in our organization, so when the time comes to stick up one of these places, we'll just use a few of them."

There was a slight knock on the door and Betty came in carrying their drinks on a tray. The men accepted them in silence.

She turned to leave, but Kenyatta stopped her. "Wait, honey, this may interest you," he stated, opening the desk drawer. "I wanted to knock the stamp place off on the first of the month, but since it's past, we'll just have to be happy with what we can get on the weekend take." He spread some blueprints out on the desk. "This is the layout of the joint. We'll send some people over to knock it off tomorrow."

Ali opened his mouth in surprise. This was the reason that people followed Kenyatta. When he made up his mind to do something, it was always done right.

3

————

THE ARMORED TRANSPORT driver cursed as he pulled up in front of the Food Stamp Collection Agency on Grand River Avenue. A tall black woman stood in front of a car with the hood up. She watched the driver closely as he pulled into a parking space two cars ahead of hers.

As soon as the truck was parked and the two guards got out, the tall woman slammed the hood of the car down. She seated herself in the car and watched the heavily armed guards as they entered the agency.

Inside the building a crowd of people seemed to be milling around, but as one's eyes became accustomed to the darkness, one realized that they were actually standing in separate lines. At the front of each line was a window with a teller behind it. There were bars over each window except at the bottom, where there was a large enough space for a man or woman to crawl through.

There was one security guard in the building and, when the two transport guards entered, he joined them.

There was a small wooden gate that led through to the other side of the windows where the women tellers worked. The guards joked with the black security guard as the trio went into the rear. The manager came out of his office and joined them.

They began at the cage farthest from the entrance door. The woman in the cage had to unlock her door from the inside to allow the men to enter. Inside it was like a small cabinet, fitted with shelves overlapping the small steel safe that contained the money. As each customer bought food stamps, the money was put in an envelope, sealed, and dropped into the safe, where it remained until the transport men picked it up twice a week.

As the manager stepped into the small cage, he removed a large key ring and inserted a key into the lock. Next, the guard stepped up and inserted his key. At this point the door swung open. Quickly the guard stuffed the money into the bag that his partner held. It didn't take long before the small safe was empty. They moved quickly to the next cage and followed the same procedure. Finally, they reached the last one.

By the time the last safe had been emptied, the guards had filled three moneybags. Sweat stood out on the forehead of the guard with the key. He was a large, red-faced man with heavy jowls, ill-fitting clothes, and a huge pot belly.

"Goddamn this heat!" he cursed, not worrying about his profanity in front of the black female worker. The fat white manager grinned at him as they worked. They were two of a kind.

"I wish I could offer you a drink, knowing how it is," the manager said as they stepped back from the cage.

From out of nowhere a black man appeared in the section behind the cages. Before anyone could react to his appearance, another one appeared at his side. Both men wore long three-quarter-length summer coats. As the stunned group of guards stared at them, the men brushed back their coats and presented the sawed-off shotguns they held in their hands.

"What the goddamn hell are you guys trying to pull?" the manager yelled angrily.

There was fear in the manager's face, but over-riding that fear was anger. He became a bright red as the blood rushed to his face.

"I won't stand still for it!" the manager yelled.

Instead of useless curse words, the heavyset transport guard went into action. He couldn't allow a stickup. It would go on his record, a mark he didn't want, and one he wouldn't have. In twenty years as a guard he had never had any money taken from him. They had attempted to five years ago, three young black boys, but he and his part-ner had handled it. They had killed two of the kids and wounded a third one. He remembered the newspapers and all the publicity. For a few days he had been a hero to the public and his every word publicized.

Those very thoughts were running through his mind when he made his foolish move. He fell to one side, trying to make that fast draw he had practiced so much, He never got his huge pistol out of the holster.

A third black man in the front of the group stepped forward, raised the short-barreled shotgun an inch, and pulled the trigger. The distance between them was less than six feet. The shot nearly cut the guard in half. It lifted him up off his feet and blew him back almost the length of the room.

The second guard didn't fare any better. He made his move at just about the same time his partner made his. The second black man in the group shot him, and the shot hit him in the face. Blood flew everywhere. Where there had been a nose and eyes, there were only gaping holes.

It should have been enough, but it wasn't. Whether or not the black security guard acted out of fear or the desire to be a hero would never be known. He tried to clear leather with his pistol, but only managed to join the other men on the floor. He clutched at his stomach, trying to hold in his guts, which were pouring out of a huge hole in his stomach.

Whether or not he realized what was about to

happen, the manager began to back up, pleading with each step he took. "Take the money," he cried, "take it all, but don't hurt me. See . . ." He raised his hands high in the air. "I'm unarmed, you guys don't have nothing to fear from me. See?" He stretched his arms even higher in the air.

As he begged, one of the black men in the rear ran past the other men towards the back of the building. He returned almost instantly. "It takes a key to open it," he yelled.

Screams of fear came from the crowd of predominantly black people in the front of the building. The black man standing in the front door holding his shotgun on them was beginning to have trouble from some of the fear-ridden women. "Stay back," he yelled loudly at them. The sounds of the shooting had just about driven them mad with fear. They pushed and shoved from the rear, until those in front were forced to move.

The gunman made up his mind at once. He didn't want to shoot any innocent people down, so he stepped aside. "Okay," he yelled out, "get the hell on." The stampede began. The women ran out the door, fighting each other in their haste to get away.

Some of them weren't so lucky. The old ones were knocked to the floor, then trampled by the frightened women behind them. Then someone shoved a terrified woman aside. The woman fell across the small counter-like shelf that kept the people away from the window. Others followed her, until there was a jammed up group inches away from the glass. Another gunshot went off, causing more bedlam, and this time the people nearest the glass couldn't push back hard enough. The ones in front went through the plate glass. Everyone was screaming in terror.

"We need the key that opens the back door," one of the holdup men yelled at the manager.

"Here, here it is," the frightened man yelled, snatching the ring loose from the small key chain. "Take it." He tossed it in their direction.

One of the men snatched up the keys and ran towards the door. The other bandit grabbed up the moneybags and ran after him. The third stickup man was undecided. He kept his gun on the manager until the fourth man reached him.

"Watch him for a second," he ordered, then ran to the rear of the building. The fourth bandit, who had been holding the crowd back from the front door, glanced down at the dead bodies lying on the floor.

"Shit!" he cursed, raising his weapon towards the manager.

The manager saw his own death in the man's cold black eyes. "Please," he begged, "please, I got a wife and k. . . ."

The blast of the sawed-off shotgun was muffled by the cries of the women. The female tellers were crouching in their cages, screaming at the death around them.

Pain exploded from the manager's chest. He

staggered from the force of the blow that struck him, but it didn't knock him off his feet. He could feel the pain even as the enveloping blackness prevented him from screaming out like the women. The blood-spattered wall held him up for a time, but the last remaining strength in his legs gave out and he crumpled up and slid to the floor.

As the murderer ran after his partners, the women inside the cages got up off the floor and fled. They were afraid the killers might come back.

Before the killer could reach the back door, he met the man who had ordered him to stay. "What did you do with the manager?" he asked quickly.

"I killed him," came the frank answer.

"Come on, then. We've got the back door opened," he stated, turning to lead the way. The man ran past him. Now there was only fear in the killers' hearts.

"Shake the lead out of your ass, Red," the man yelled back over his shoulder. "The fuckin' police will be all over this joint in a minute."

The man called Red didn't answer but just followed on the fleeing man's heels. When they reached the alley, the same car that had been stalled in front of the building was waiting.

Betty sat behind the steering wheel impatiently. She gunned the motor as the last of the men came out. They had hardly jumped in before she had the car in motion and was pulling away. The gravel in the alley flying from under the speeding car's wheels was the only sound heard inside the car as they made their getaway. The alley ended where another alley crossed. This was where Betty made her turn, taking a left.

There was clear driving down the long, empty alleyway. Betty slowed down slightly and drove at a more moderate pace.

As they passed a vacant garage, two boys came out and put four garbage cans across the alley. If there was any pursuit, the occupants of the following cars would have to get out and clear away the cans.

Betty smiled to herself as she watched them disappear in her mirror. Kenyatta thought of everything, she reflected as she drove even slower. That slight glimpse of the boys protecting their rear filled her with a confidence she hadn't had earlier. When she had first heard the gunshots going off inside the building, her first thought had been of fleeing. She had a hard time fighting down the desire to leave. They must have gotten busted inside. What other reason for all the shooting, she'd asked herself.

She came to the end of the alley and stopped. She glanced both ways before pulling out into the traffic. When they reached the next intersection, a police car came flying past, heading for Grand River Avenue. She waited for the speeding police car to cross in front of them.

"They must be on a code three," someone said from the backseat.

The sound of his voice breaking the silence also helped break the tension. The rest of the people in the car cracked up laughing.

"Goddamn, Eddie-Bee," Red said, holding his side. "Leave it up to you, man, and you'll make a funny on your way to hell."

The slim, brown-skinned man called Eddie-Bee smiled slightly. It made him feel good to make people laugh. It was one of the few things he really enjoyed in life, trying to be a comic.

Betty glanced over at Red sitting in the front seat next to her. "How did everything go?" she asked quietly. "You know, I heard all that damn shootin', so I'm sure as hell curious about it."

"I'll just bet your ass is," Red replied. "It's enough to make you curious." He stopped and twisted around in the car seat. "Our boy Zeke here started the ball to rolling," he began. "The fool-ass guard tried to go for his gun and Zeke sent him to see his maker."

The tall, slim, brown-skinned Negro sitting by the rear window moved nervously in his seat.

"Look here, brother," he began, speaking slowly. "I don't mind Betty knowing about it because she was up on the robbery with us. But after this, let's not do any mentioning of who shot who, okay?" he said seriously. "I know I ain't got nothing to worry about because all of us just about killed somebody back there, but I'm talking about when we get back to our club, let's not speak of who shot who."

"I'll go along with that," the short, plump man sitting between Eddie-Bee and Zeke stated. "There was too much bloodshed back there for us to talk about it. Them kind of things are best left untalked about."

"Don't worry, Charles," Red said casually. "Even though everybody in our club is cool, it is better not to talk about it. I'd even go as far as to say, don't even mention that you were on the job. Just being up on it is enough to get all day in prison."

Everybody in the car agreed with Red. Robert, the man who had run past Red so fast, gave a short laugh. "Shit, Red, as slow as you were moving, I'd have thought you kind of wanted to get cracked out. You know what they say, once a guy has spent as much time in Jackson as you have, he becomes institutionalized to such a degree that he really misses that way of life."

Red laughed along with the rest of the people. "Naw, baby, but havin' a foot race with you to see who got out first wouldn't have been cool either. Just like your running past me wasn't the coolest thing in the world."

Robert started to argue, but Red cut him off. "Kenyatta asked me to be in charge to a certain degree, you know, so I felt it was my duty to see that everything went off right. You ain't forgot, have you, Robert, that I was on my way back in just to get you?"

For just a minute, Robert looked around sheepishly, then he regained his bravado. "Yeah, I know

you were, but you ain't forgot either that you ordered me to stay there to the last and watch that
fat-ass banker."

"Goddamn it," Charles cried out, "I meant to
put a slug or two into his fat ass. I hate a whitey
who looks like that bastard. I mean, you can actually tell he's a flunky motherfucker on a black nigger's ass."

"Well, you don't have to worry about him no
more. That's one honky that won't be giving out
any more orders, unless it's in hell."

Betty turned onto a side street. "I hope you done
put them guns and money inside those shoppin'
bags," she said as she pulled up beside a small compact car. Inside was a woman who looked as if she
was white.

The woman glanced up and down the street
anxiously as Betty parked beside her. "Hi, Arlene,"
Betty yelled as Red slipped out of the car and took
the keys from Arlene. He went around and opened
up the trunk of her car and put the shopping bags
inside. When he came back, he removed the trunk
key from the ring before giving the keys back to
the woman.

"Well, we'll be seeing you around, honey," Betty
called out sweetly as she pulled away. She watched
in the mirror as Arlene drove off. "Well, that takes
care of that. Arlene is so light that, if the police
should stop her, she won't have no trouble because
they'll think she's a white girl and let her go."

"That's sure enough cool, but what's cooler

yet," Zeke said from the back, "is that we ain't got that hot shit in the car with us no more."

"Amen," Robert said. "You can sure as hell say amen to that!"

When Betty stopped at another intersection a police car cruised past them slowly. The driver gave them the once-over, but seeing a woman driving must have thrown him off because he kept on going.

"I'll say amen, amen, loud and clear now," Red said, and they all laughed. They knew now that they could really relax. They were home clear. There was no more need to fear a bust. Everything had been taken care of.

4

INSIDE THE WELL-FURNISHED six-room apartment over the club were the people who had participated in the robbery. Kenyatta counted the money for the third time, then, after removing fifteen thousand dollars, made six small piles of money. He gave each person who had been involved in the robbery two thousand dollars. Nobody complained about the way he split it up.

"I for one," he said earnestly, "am damn glad that this shit is over with." Kenyatta glanced around at the smiling faces. "I guess just about everybody is happy, huh?"

Red tossed off a shot glass of whiskey before speaking. They had been drinking and toasting each other since early that morning. "That ain't the half of it," he said, his voice sounding hard and cold. "I hope that finished it up for good. I hate robberies of any kind. That's why it's a shame Billy and Jackie ain't still around. They loved to knock over shit like that."

Kenyatta studied him closely before speaking. "You're one-hundred-percent correct about that, Red, 'cause that joint happened to be Billy's pet project. He'd been trying to talk me into knocking off that particular joint for damn near a year."

As he spoke, Kenyatta noticed Betty weaving through the living room, clutching a drink in her hand. He was momentarily surprised to see her stagger. He'd never before seen her drink enough to get loaded. She dropped into his lap, then rolled her beautiful eyes up at him. He noticed that they were bloodshot. He had a deep conviction that the past few weeks had put her under too much pressure. The only reason he'd sent her on the robbery was because he'd wanted her to do something that would take her mind off her Auntie Joy's death. There had been no way for him to foresee that the robbery would turn into a bloodbath.

He squeezed her small waist tightly. "Enjoying yourself, honey?" he inquired in what she termed his passionate bedroom voice.

Betty smiled up at him, her face lighting up and her pearly-white teeth gleaming. "You better damn well believe it. I didn't know Johnnie Walker Black could make you feel so good."

As Red stood up to go, he staggered. "I believe I'll be gettin' on down the road," he said, picking up his money. "I got a date with an angel." He attempted to sing, but Kenyatta cut him off.

"Why don't you leave some of your cash here, Red? You don't need all that money in the streets with you at one time."

It seemed as if he might comply with Kenyatta's wishes as he stood there rocking back and forth, but the alcohol got the best of him. "Hey, baby boy, why you come down on me like that? I ain't no kid, you know. I can well take care of myself, brother."

This is the kind of shit that blows everything up in a man's face, Kenyatta thought coldly as he watched the man reel.

"I can take care of myself," Red repeated. Then he reached inside his shirt and came out with a pistol. "See, Ken, I ain't going in the goddamn street without some kind of help, brother. I wish a motherfucker would try and take something away from me." He waved the gun at the couple sitting in the chairs.

Kenyatta gritted his teeth. He knew exactly what he was going to have to do. There was no sense in wasting his time trying to talk the man out of his drunken plans. Kenyatta knew from past experience that, once Red started to drink, he was bullheaded and hard to reason with. Even trying to talk him out of the pistol would be a senseless effort.

Kenyatta hated what he was about to do. He tried to make his mind a blank and stifle any thoughts, because he knew he'd be arguing with himself. Who the hell was he to try to play God? The man had earned the money, so why not let him go out and spend it any way he wanted to? His answer to himself was that the man would probably end up shooting somebody. He would have to disarm him.

Kenyatta raised up out of the chair and set Betty down on her feet. "Come on, bro," he said, friendly like, "I'll walk you to the front door. I got something I want to talk to you about anyway."

Red grinned at him foolishly, then started to put the gun away. The punch came at him swiftly. It was short and explosive. If Red had been just a little bit more sober, he would have ducked it. As it was, he almost rolled away from it, revealing how well Kenyatta had trained his people. The blow caught Red on the jaw. He dropped and slowly crumpled up on the floor, knocked completely out.

"I knew it," Charles said from where he sat. "I couldn't believe you were going to let him go in the streets like that."

"I hated to do it," Kenyatta explained to the people watching, "but we got too much to lose to allow him to run around in the streets drunk. If the police get him, no telling what he might say while under the influence of that shit, so it's better all the way around if he stays right here until he's sober."

Kenyatta stopped, reached down, and removed the pistol from the drunken man's coat pocket.

"That's a funky thing to do," Betty said as her whiskey began to talk for her. "Shit, what did Red do to deserve all that?" She glared around angrily. "I don't care if all the rest of these niggers are scared of you, Kenyatta, but I'm sure in the hell not." She belched loudly.

"Shit, Kenyatta," Zeke said from where he sat on the couch nursing his small glass of wine, "looks like you might have another one to go."

"Okay, yeah," she snarled as she staggered around the table to get a better look at Zeke. "Why don't you kill-crazy bastards just kill me, huh? Wouldn't that be the easy way out for all of you? Hell, I know too much for you to let me go on living, don't I? So just shoot me, right here in the top of the head," she said, pointing out the spot.

Her words had brought a snap of fear to most of the people in the room. They were too involved in the robbery to have someone come up with a loose lip. They glanced up at Kenyatta to see how he was taking his woman's words. This could turn into one hell of a dilemma if Kenyatta didn't get her mind right.

He raised his hand, asking for silence. "I know what most of you are thinkin', but forget it. This is the first time any of you have ever seen her drunk, and I promise you it will be the last," he said, not realizing that he was making a promise he would not be able to keep.

"Hey, brother," Robert called out, "we know how it is, man. Just like you said, I ain't never seen Betty loaded before, I mean never. Not even close, man, so I know it's just the drinks in her talking." He spoke with conviction, because he really liked the tall black woman.

"Technically speaking," Eddie-Bee began, loaded enough himself to start trying to talk proper, which he did whenever he reached a certain point in his drinking, "I'd say we've all had a few too many, but that's why we started drinking, wasn't it? Weren't we supposed to be celebrating something or other? So what the fuck. Let's let our hair hang loose. It's exhilarating to be loaded around friends." He stopped and took a large drink from the paper cup in front of him, then continued. "I'm ready to call the ladies up from downstairs myself. Let's party, dig? We're not here to merely exist, are we?" He glared around at his friends, then spoke to Betty directly. "I really sympathize with you, Betty. It's getting increasingly boring up here." He tried to turn his back but only succeeded in knocking his cup of whiskey onto the thick brown carpet.

The other men laughed. But as Kenyatta took Betty into his arms, she started a crying jag. At first she cried softly, then the sobs came louder and louder. He glanced around at the other men nervously, then reached down and picked her up and carried her to the bedroom. Once there, he covered her lips with hot kisses, holding her tight and slowly rubbing her back as if she was a nervous filly. She settled down slowly, and he could tell she was coming around and relaxing. Her lips grew softer under his, her tongue came out to meet his until there was nothing but a strong passion between them. After undressing her with care, he took her. They made slow and tender love. Her cries of fear turned into cries of passion.

5

CAPTAIN DAVIDSON STARED over his horn-rimmed glasses at the two officers in front of him. The stout, graying officer realized that it wasn't their fault that none of the officers in homicide had cracked the case yet. At least these two men had come closer to getting an arrest than any of the others. But he still had to crack the whip over their heads, just as he did with the rest of the men.

"Goddamn it, Ryan, Benson, what the hell are you two guys doing back there in your office? Playing with yourselves?" He waited for a second, then continued in a bullish voice. "I can expect nothing from these young college-ass kids I'm stuck with in this department, but you two guys, shit!" The word came out in a roar. It could be heard out front, where all the junior officers worked.

Ryan shifted nervously on his feet. He couldn't stand being yelled at. It caused his nerves to work overtime, like they were doing now.

Benson only fought down the smile that threatened to come to his lips. He realized how nervous Ryan must be by the loud yelling of their boss. That was the reason Ryan couldn't stand the interviews. The yelling just upset him until he couldn't think straight.

Davidson must have realized that he was overdoing it because he lowered his voice. "Now fellows," he began, trying another approach, "let's try and look at it from my side of the wagon, okay? The fuckin' commissioner is breathing down my neck, cops literally gettin' killed at will. And now this. Two men with their girlfriends murdered in cold blood in broad daylight, yet nobody saw anything. It's unbelievable. I mean it. We're not back in the roaring twenties. These things just don't go on in our day and age without getting solved, so what's the problem? I don't want to hear about won't nobody talk. I gave you guys a free hand, allowing you to work when you wanted to."

He raised his hand to cut off an excuse from Ryan. "Yeah, I know. You boys were going to work on your own time. I appreciate the offer, but what did I do? I said no sirree, not on your own time. Just punch in, and I'd see to it that you're paid for every fuckin' minute you put in down here, didn't I?"

Before the men could reply, he continued, and his voice rose higher. "Now, you can't beat such a boss, can you? I put my fat ass out on the limb for you guys. And now they're trying to cut the fuckin' limb off while I'm out on it. But I promise you guys one thing, if they cut it off on me, I'll make damn sure I fall on somebody's head before I hit the ground. Do I make myself clear?"

Both of the officers shook their heads in agreement, thankful that the interview was over and not really bothered by the threat. Before Davidson got rid of them, a hell of a lot of other officers would feel his heavy hand. They were the closest ones to the case. No other team of detectives was anywhere nearer to solving the murder spree than they were.

"Oh, Benson, Ryan," Davidson called out as the two men neared the door in their rush to get clear of the captain's office, "the next time I send you guys two young detectives to take along, please take them. How the hell else are these guys going to get any experience if they don't go with some of you vets?"

"That was my fault, Captain," Benson said quickly. "I. . . ."

The captain waved the excuse away. "I didn't ask about whose fault it was; just take them along next time. I don't see how they can get in the way by just riding in the backseat of a fuckin' police car."

"Okay, Captain, we'll take care of it," Benson replied as he opened the door.

Ryan almost ran through the open door in his haste to get away from the captain. As they made their way through the office, Benson noticed the two young detectives sitting at the desk. Both men were grinning.

As Benson caught their eyes, the men glanced away, but not before he could see the look of triumph.

"Up your fuckin' ass," Benson said under his breath. He promised himself that it would be a cold day in hell before he'd allow those bastards to follow him along on any case.

"Hey, Ryan," a slim, red-faced detective called out as they passed, "you and Ben had better check and see if you've still got anything back there to sit on."

The other officers sitting nearby broke out laughing. It tickled them to see another man on the carpet, just as long as it wasn't their own asses catching the hell. To get called into the captain's office wasn't anything to be proud of. He very seldom wanted to see an officer unless it was about something important on a new case, or about someone's mistake.

Benson glared around defiantly at the white officers. It didn't take much for him to realize that they enjoyed what they thought was his being put into place. But a hell of a lot of people had been killed lately, and not only hadn't Ryan and Benson had any luck, but neither had any of the other detectives in the room.

"Let's take a quick ride," Ryan said briskly, not even waiting for his partner's answer. He kept walking until they got in the elevator, then pushed the button for the garage.

Both men remained silent, trying to make some kind of sense out of the latest murders. Ryan drove, taking the freeway until he reached the Clay Street exit. He took the ramp that led to the right and made a turn over to Oakland Avenue. He parked behind a moving van, then removed a small slip of paper from his pocket.

"Kenyatta," he said out loud. "I don't know if he's got anything to do with this shit, but everything we've got leads in his direction."

Benson nodded toward the storefront a few cars away. "Well, that's the bastard's funky-ass club. It took a hell of a lot of trouble just to get somebody to have the nerve to tell us where it was located," Benson stated, then continued. "That in itself speaks of the enormous ghetto power. Whenever people fear somebody, as it seems these people fear him, it's time we looked into it."

Ryan nodded his head in agreement. "I can't understand how this guy exploded in our midst without us ever gettin' any kind of wire on him.

It's as if he came from another world. Nobody, and I mean nobody, wants to talk about him or his people."

As the two detectives sat watching the front of the club, a small black Ford pulled up. The car was tilted over towards the driver's seat, and when the driver got out, it was easy to see why. A huge, fat, white man got out from the driver's side and waddled around the car, carrying a brown briefcase in his left hand. He glanced down at a piece of paper in his right hand, reading an address as he reached the sidewalk.

The three black men loitering in front of the building stared at him coldly as he pushed past them. He was breathing hard as though he had just run ten miles.

"I wonder who the hell he could be," Benson said quietly.

Ryan lifted his shoulders in a shrug. "He could be the neighborhood's friendly insurance man, you know." Even while he was talking, Ryan was writing down the license number of the late-model car.

As Benson watched his partner write down the number, he couldn't help but think how it would be if the fat white man had been black. His partner probably would have suggested that they pull him over when he came out and shake him down.

For spite, Benson started to make the suggestion himself. Why not, he thought coldly. What's good for a black man should be good for a white one, too. But he knew better. If the white man turned out to be a working businessman going about his business of robbing the black neighborhood and they shook him down, all he'd have to do would be to call downtown and make a complaint about being illegally stopped and searched. Then there would be hell to pay, They would have to come up with some kind of an excuse for why they had detained the man and put him through so much trouble.

Benson had to laugh sardonically as he thought about it: all those black men who were stopped daily, even with their wives along, and searched out on the streets for no other reason than that they were black. The officers who stopped them believed all black men did something wrong, so they had a right to stop and frisk any black man they saw. But it was so different when it came to a white man. *Oh God, so much different,* he moaned.

"What's wrong?" Ryan inquired slowly, studying his partner closely. "You got an idea or something?"

For just a minute Benson debated with himself on whether or not to let his partner in on his private little joke.

Defiantly he stated, "Oh man, do you really want to know?" He then continued before Ryan could answer, "I was thinking, Ryan, why go through the trouble of writing his number down, then havin' to check it downtown, when more than fuckin' likely it's a rented car in a phony name? To beat all that shit, why don't we just act like he's a black dude when he comes out and lean on him a little. You know what I mean, Ryan? We lean on enough niggers daily for it to be quite easy."

Benson watched his partner's face. It went red, then Ryan rubbed at his chin nervously, trying to make up his mind on how to answer Benson.

"Man, you're really in a hell of a mood today, huh?" Ryan began as he thought over the ticklish question Benson had dropped in his lap. He cursed silently at himself, wishing he had left well enough alone. Now, since he'd asked for it, Benson had really put it in his lap. All of the problems of what could happen flashed through his mind. The last thing he wanted was another meeting with the captain—not anytime soon anyway. If the fat salesman was to do any complaining, that's just what it would add up to. Another fuckin' meeting with the captain. There was something like a tacit agreement among the policemen about white businessmen. You didn't harass them while they were down in the black neighborhoods. A white junkie was something else. He was nothing. But a taxpayer, that was a horse of another color— white color at that.

Benson could read it all in his face. "Don't worry,

Ryan, I was just foolin' with you, man. I don't want the trouble it could bring either."

For a minute Ryan couldn't look his partner in the eye. "You make me feel like a three-dollar bill, Ben. If you want to, we can shake him down. I was just thinking, though, if a kickback comes out of this shit, we'll have some tall explaining to do. The fuckin' captain will say, 'Why are you guys hustling a white man? Everybody in the city knows it was black gunmen who made the hit, so where's the connection with this white merchant?'"

He didn't have to illustrate too much for Benson to know that his partner was right. "I mean, Ben," Ryan added, "it won't go as hard for me as it could go for you. All I'd have to say was that it was your idea and I just went along with it, even though you know I wouldn't shift the blame on you. But I'm just trying to show you where we'd be. The first thing we'd have to answer is why. Why in the fuck did we bother him? Don't we have enough troublemakers down here to cope with without going out of our way to disturb workin' people?"

The very air in the car seemed to become oppressive to Benson, but what his partner said was true. They would never be able to make their superiors understand. Even as Benson thought about it, it seemed foolish. What would a well-dressed white man want with someone like Kenyatta, except to sell him something that would be junk a month later? They lived in two different worlds; the world of men like Kenyatta was a black world, devoid of whites. Even as Benson thought about it, he remembered that the little he was able to dig up on Kenyatta showed him to be militant, preaching against associating with whites. As he went over the possibilities in his mind, Benson quickly came to the conclusion that the fat white man was probably just the landlord coming to collect his rent.

He put his thoughts into words. "You know, Ryan, I'm grabbing at straws, really. That guy's probably the landlord trying to collect his rent." Benson laughed dryly, then added, "And that's more than likely one hell of a job right there, trying to get his rent out of a bunch of hustlers like them punks hanging out there. Yeah, he's got one hell of a job on his hands, if I know anything about young brothers."

Ryan wasn't fooled by his partner's words. It had hurt Benson to make that small confession. Benson really wanted to shake down the white man. "Now, Ben, don't go against your hunches. If you want to, just give the word, man, and we'll have that fat load of lard jacked up before God gets the news."

"You're a good man, Ryan," Benson said slowly. "Yeah, you're a damn good one to work with. But now that I think about it, I believe I was wrong. I can't picture no reason for there to be any connection between them, other than legal business. Kenyatta hates whites, so they couldn't have much other than business between them. Let's let it pass this time. We can still check out the license number with headquarters."

6

THE BLACK MEN SHUFFLED reluctantly out of Kenyatta's private office. None of them wanted to leave until they found out what the fat white man wanted. It was the first time any of them had ever seen Kenyatta treat a white man with any kind of respect. When this one entered, Kenyatta had gotten up and walked across the carpeted floor to throw his arm around the fat man's shoulders as if they were old war buddies. After making the man as comfortable as possible, Kenyatta had started ushering the rest of the people out of the office until there wasn't anyone left but him and the white man.

"Well, Angelo," Kenyatta began, I hope you brought what I wanted."

Angelo rubbed his hand across his huge stomach. He had been nervous at the sight of so many young, wild-looking black men. He knew they were followers of Kenyatta, and that Kenyatta preached death to the white man. So far, though, all he'd received was the red-carpet treatment.

Before answering the question Kenyatta had put to him, he asked one of his own. "What about the paper? You know what I mean, that green stuff." Angelo leaned across the desk on his elbows and tried to stare Kenyatta in the eye but quickly changed his mind. Instead he tried to cover up his error by playing the big shot.

"I don't generally come this far out of my way for no fuckin' body, Kenny," he stated, glaring across the desk, "but you've been bugging me for this information for the past six months at least, so I come up with it for you, but I've got to have my bread."

Kenyatta stared coldly at the nervous white man. Suddenly he stood up from behind his desk. "Listen, sucker," he began loudly, "you come down here and I try and treat you like a man, but that ain't good enough for you. You want us to kiss your fuckin' ass to show how much we appreciate your coming *down* here, as you say. But we ain't doing nothing of the kind. Honky, you came *down* here because you can't sell that information you got nowhere else in this world. Ain't nobody willin' to pay the price I was goin' pay for it."

Angelo drew a deep breath, letting it out slowly,

hoping the tightness he felt would disappear with it. He hadn't missed the past tense Kenyatta had used. The words seemed to stifle the very air in the room. He pulled at his collar, and his face became red as a beet. The glare coming from the ceiling lights seemed to move the walls inward, sealing him in. He could picture the army of people he was in debt to, marching arm in arm toward him, each one carrying a different kind of weapon.

"Now wait a minute, boy," he began, and realized at once that he had blundered before he even began. That was the problem of trying to deal with these fuckin' spades. You couldn't open your mouth without steppin' on their tender egos some kind of way.

Kenyatta's voice was smooth and softly triumphant. "Things have just changed a little, that's all, Angelo. We don't have to pay that wild price you were asking now because we already know half of the names ourselves. But," Kenyatta waved to the man to remain silent, "since you did go through so much trouble, we've decided to offer you five thousand dollars for your snitching. I mean, if you really look at it like you should, that's good money for an informer, whether he's white or black."

Being called an informer didn't set too well with Angelo either, but what hurt worse than that was the thought that he couldn't collect the whole ten thousand dollars he had come to think of as his own. Yet five grand was better than nothing. As far as he was concerned, the information he was passing on to these black guys was less than useless. He couldn't see what they could possibly do with it. Even if they turned it over to the police, it would be nothing new. The big wheels in the police department already knew who was responsible for the steady flow of dope into the city, yet they couldn't, or wouldn't, do anything about it. So what could some black hoods living in a ghetto do?

Angrily he reached in his pocket and snatched out the envelope. "Here," he snarled as he tossed it across the desk, all the time hoping that the black man wouldn't change his mind again. He needed the five grand to live. Without it, he was a walking dead man. His mind was already working on how he could pay certain people half their money. When they saw him come up with some cash, they would know that he was trying, that he wasn't just attempting to shine them on. Yes, the five grand would be enough to hold back the strong-arm boys.

Kenyatta stared at the envelope as if it was a snake. He hadn't appreciated the white man tossing it down on his desk instead of handing it to him like a man. For a second, he visualized himself choking the fat man to death. It was a picture that he enjoyed. How desperately the fat man would struggle. The image of the man's red face turning blue brought a smile to his lips.

Angelo sat impatiently waiting for Kenyatta to make up his mind. Nervously he lit up a fat cigar. "I mean, what the hell gives around here, Kenyatta? We ain't never had any kind of misunderstanding like this before. I bring you what you ask for, but you've changed the fuckin' price. How the hell will you feel if I should do the same thing to you the next time you put in a big order for guns, huh?"

It didn't take a mind reader to see that he had hit on a vital organ. The steady supply of fresh, untraceable guns was indispensable. It was of the greatest importance that Kenyatta keep his gun connection. Angelo saw this and pushed home his point. "You and me, Kenyatta, we been doing business for over two years now, without ever having any trouble. Now, all at once, here comes some bullshit. Okay, I accept the fact that ten grand was too much money for the information you wanted, but don't rub my nose in shit, boy."

There it was again, that fuckin' term "boy." Kenyatta gritted his teeth before jumping up and stalking around the desk. "Angelo, I'm goin' tell you one time, man, and only once. The way you honkies have of calling us 'boy' is too much. I'm one nigger who just can't stand it. Now, I know you probably don't mean a fuckin' thing by it, but it still rubs me to the quick to hear a peckerwood call me 'boy,' so you done run out of chances. If you do it again, no matter how bad I might need your gun connect, I'll personally kick you in your fat ass until all the lard runs off it."

All the while the tall black man spoke, he pointed his finger down into the white man's face. Angelo could only sit in the chair and stare up at him with his mouth open. He promised himself though, if he got out of that office alive, it would be a cold day in hell before he'd ever come down near the ghetto and do business with the black bastards again. Oh yes, he'd continue to sell them guns. It made him feel good to know that he was supplying the guns they were killing each other with. In time, maybe they'd kill so many of their brothers that the white people could start getting back some parts of the cities because, the way things stood, niggers had already taken over the major portions.

"I didn't mean no harm, Kenyatta; it's just that I forget how to pronounce your name at times and 'boy' comes out. But don't worry, I won't make that mistake again."

Kenyatta glared down at the man without smiling. "I ain't worried about it at all," Kenyatta said. "I've already warned you; the rest is up to you." He turned his back on the fat man and walked back around his desk. This time he did pick up the envelope. He opened it quickly, glanced down at the names, then back up at Angelo. "What kind of shit is this you're giving me, Angelo? You got the Kingfisher in charge of the dope on the west side, east side, north side, and south side of the city. In other words, you got a black man in charge of all the dope that goes into the ghettos."

Angelo held up his hand, catching himself before he made the mistake of calling Kenyatta boy. "It's the goddamn truth. I was surprised as hell when I found it out. I didn't know a nigger had that much power." He became tongue-tied as he suddenly realized the word he had used, but since no warning came he continued. "It's the truth though. Kingfisher has the whole ball of wax. There's not a white distributor in the whole fuckin' city who can put any dope in the ghettos without the okay of the Kingfisher."

Angelo's words rang in Kenyatta's ears. "That's the way that bastard has got it set up. No drugs are sold on the large levels unless he has something to do with it. It's no big outlet in the suburbs yet, so the big boys have to play to the Kingfisher's tune for now. They damn sure don't like it, but what can they do about it? There's not another colored guy around anywhere as big as the Kingfisher. He don't allow it. If the big white boys try and set up another black guy, something always seems to happen to the guy. It's a short investment, so they have to do business with the Kingfisher."

The spectacle of watching the facial expressions of Kenyatta was enough to scare the shit out of

some people, and Angelo was no exception. At
first Kenyatta had been defiant, then uncontrolled
fury flashed across his features. Just the mention
of the Kingfisher was enough to make Angelo
wish he was somewhere else.

"Well," Angelo began, "I'd appreciate it if we
closed our little business deal, because I've got to
get uptown and check on a shipment of guns. You
do still want that big order, don't you?" It was
clear he was trying desperately to change the subject.

With difficulty Kenyatta managed to bring his
mind back to the business at hand. A blinding white
rage had blotted out all his thoughts for a moment, until the only thing he could think about
was revenge.

But the guns were of immediate concern to him.
Without them, he couldn't begin to put into prac-
tice any of the far-reaching plans he had. It took a
few seconds but he managed to gain control of
his anger.

"Yeah, Angelo, I know where you're coming
from. Just hold on to your shirt for a minute, man,"
he said, as he reached inside his pocket and removed an envelope. He took his time and counted
out the money on the desk. Angelo counted the
money alongside him, not even attempting to keep
the greed out of his eyes.

"Why don't you give me a partial payment
down on the guns now, Ken, and tomorrow night

when you send your people over to pick them up, they won't have to have that much cash on them." Angelo's eyes continued to follow the large roll of money still inside the envelope.

Kenyatta laughed loudly. "Man, you must really need some bread bad, Angelo. Suppose I did what you asked me to do, then something happened during the pickup. I'd be out of my money, plus the guns. No, baby, ain't no way for it to go like that. I couldn't stand to lose on both ends. It would hurt me bad enough if the cops knocked off our pickup spot, but it would ruin me if I lost all my bankroll along with it." The tall, lean, black man stood up from behind his desk, showing by his actions that the interview was over. He walked around the desk and took Angelo's arm, leading the white man toward the door. "To show you how much I'm concerned about you, Angelo, I'm even going to walk you out to your car so that there won't be no chance of somebody knockin' you off for the few bucks you just picked up. I don't want no shit out of you, you know what I mean? Like you calling me back in an hour tellin' me some shit about somebody knockin' you over. Well, baby, I'm goin' make damn sure that don't happen."

The black man's deep laughter boomed out loudly as they went through the outer office. Neither man took notice of the black men standing around in the room.

Near the front window, two Negro men stood peeping out. One of them yelled out to Kenyatta before he opened the front door. "Hey, baby, maybe you had better be cool. It's a couple of detectives parked down the street. They been there ever since fat boy pulled up and parked. At first we thought they might have been a couple of his boys, you know, trying to put a little protection on him, but we checked them out and it's them two detectives from homicide. The black and white cops that always work together."

Kenyatta stopped with his hand on the door, undecided on which course to take. "You say they been down there checkin' out the place, huh?" he asked, his mind racing.

"Naw," the tall, angular black man called Jug replied. "Naw, I didn't say they were checkin' out our joint. I said they seemed to be checkin' out fat boy's car."

As Jug talked, Angelo stared at the black man. He shook his head. They did all look alike, only this one had hair. If he cut off his hair, he'd probably look just like Kenyatta, Angelo reasoned quietly.

It was true to a certain extent. Kenyatta and Jug were almost the same height; both men had the same lean build, with wide shoulders tapering down to a small waist—men built for power, speed, and explosive action.

"Goddamn it, Kenyatta, I told you you should have come downtown and picked up that shit. Now I'm involved down here with the fuckin' po-

lice. It's been years, man, since I've had a run-in with a cop. Now, I don't need this kind of shit, but what am I going to do? I sure in the fuck can't sit here at your place all fuckin' day."

It was the man's tone of voice that rubbed him wrong. Now, even though the law was outside, Kenyatta wanted to get rid of the fat white man. He glanced over his shoulder, then snapped his fingers.

"Betty!" he ordered, his voice full of wrath.

The tall black woman came running across the room.

"Honey, I want you to walk this honky out to his car, put your arm around him, you know, give the impression that he just finished knockin' off some black pussy. The cops are down the block and we would like to fake them out, so make it look good."

She glanced up at him in surprise. "Okay, honey, you know I wanna do whatever you want me to."

It was clear to everybody looking that what Betty was doing was something Kenyatta sure in the hell didn't like. He had to turn his back when she took Angelo's arm and went out the door.

Kenyatta stalked back to his office and slammed the door. He didn't want to be bothered by anyone. Kenyatta gritted his teeth so hard his jaw hurt. It was the first time he'd ever had to use his woman in such a way. He'd rather have had her kill Angelo than walk out pretending that the fat man was her lover.

Betty led the fat man outside. She put her arm around his huge waist and held him close. She sniffed, then tried to hold her breath. There was an odor about the heavy man that was repugnant to her. It would have been farcical for her to pretend that she didn't smell him, because she couldn't hide her reaction. She pulled away from him quickly, even though she still kept her arm around his waist. But one glance at her face, with her nose turned up, would have been enough for anyone to see the dislike on it.

As obvious as it was, it went unnoticed by Angelo. He was too concerned with the police car parked down the street. He fumbled in his pockets until he found his car keys, then he attempted to make a convivial social impression for the officers watching. He puckered up his ruddy pink lips and tried to kiss Betty, but she wasn't having any of it. She didn't even want the man to kiss her on the cheek. She broke away from his embrace.

"It don't take all that," she stated coldly as she backed away from him, still smiling and grinning. The smile never touched her cold black eyes.

"Well, I'll be a sonofabitch," Benson growled

harshly. "Here we fuck up half the morning waiting on this bastard, and all the time he's upstairs playing house with one of Kenyatta's whores!"

Ryan cursed loudly too. "It looks that way, don't it? He probably came to collect the rent and the broad gave him some cunt for the rent money."

The two detectives watched the fat man drive past them slowly. It seemed as if he was trying to remove some lipstick from his cheek with a hankie as he went past.

"Well, what now?" Ryan asked quietly, deep in thought. Something was wrong, but for the moment he couldn't seem to put his finger on it.

"I don't know," Benson replied. "Maybe it would be better if we went on in. I think I'll go home and have some sleep. We seem to be too close to something not to be gettin' any answers."

Ryan shook his head. "It's right before us, Ben, but for some damn reason we can't see it. Maybe you're right. After some rest, we might be able to think better. Drop me off at my place, will you?"

Benson nodded his head in agreement. "I'll pick you back up tonight, say around ten o'clock." Neither man bothered to speak again until Benson pulled up on Carpenter Street and let his partner out.

"We missed something, Ben," Ryan stated, shaking his head. "I don't know what the fuck it was, but I just got the feelin' that something escaped us that shouldn't have."

"Maybe," Benson replied. "After you sleep on it, it might come to you." He grinned, then put the car in gear and pulled away from the curb. Even as he drove, the same thought kept nagging him; then it hit him like a ton of bricks.

Kenyatta was a black militant. There was no way in the world he would allow one of his black women to try turning a trick with a honky. They just wouldn't do it. His group preached against the white man, so it had been all a fake-out— something to fool the two foolish cops sitting down the street.

He slammed on his brakes and made a U-turn, It was too important to pass up. Ryan had the license number of the fat man's car, and he needed it. It looked as if there wouldn't be much sleep that afternoon for either one of the detectives. This clue was too good to pass up, and the case was too hot to not follow up each and every fucking thing they got their hands on.

When he pulled up in front of Ryan's house, he just blew on the horn. In seconds his partner came out of the freshly painted white house.

Ryan must have sensed something, because he ran down the battleship-gray-colored steps. When he reached the car, he didn't bother with just putting his head through the open window. He opened the door and got in. In a second, Benson explained why he had come back.

As Benson talked, Ryan nodded his head up and down. "I knew it," the man exploded. "It was there, right there before us, but neither one of us could put our finger on it at the time. Well, quit wasting time. Let's get downtown, This fat bastard had better be clean, 'cause we're going to do a lot of checkin' up on his ass."

7

AS KENYATTA STARED at the death list in his hands he could feel a thrill of exhilaration racing through his veins. Now they could do more than just merely exist. The five grand he had paid out for it was nothing. Money meant very little to him anyway. It was just a tool, something to use to gain the things he wanted for his people. Now they could begin to move against the dope pushers, the ones who supplied the city, not just the neighborhood pushers who sold dope to take care of their own drug habits.

He glanced around the apartment. He had sent out the word and the people were arriving. Loud, raucous laughter came from the front room, where a group of people waited. It was time, and everybody could sense it. The members were in a happy, responsive mood. Kenyatta had sent out the word that they were to meet at the ranch and everybody was moving to the country again.

There was a cacophony of sound coming from the people in all the rooms. It was an atmosphere of social gaiety as everybody looked forward to the trip. Some cars had already left so that things would be ready when the main party arrived at the farm.

Betty sat on the arm rest of the overstuffed chair in the living room next to Kenyatta, smiling broadly at everybody.

"Eddie-Bee," Kenyatta called out loudly. "Hey, Eddie-Bee, I thought you took the station wagon around to Johnnie's to get the starter fixed on it."

"I did, baby, I did, but wasn't no reason for me to sit around there and wait for them to finish workin' on it. Johnnie said he'd call as soon as he finished workin' on it and that Buick he's puttin' a muffler on. I told him we wanted both of them finished as soon as goddamn possible, so he said to give him thirty or forty minutes and he'd have them together for us."

Kenyatta replied by flashing Eddie-Bee one of his most indulgent smiles. "My man," he said loudly, "that's what I dig about the brothers in this organization. Ain't no bullshit about them. All of you have been trained. You're together, ready to cope with the white man, while the other brothers out in the streets are still blinded by the white man's shit."

As he talked, Kenyatta raised his voice into a

lecturing tone. "Each and every one of you in this room right now has been trained until you're like a machine—dangerous to those who try to handle you and handle you wrong."

The people in the room fell silent, listening to their leader. What he said was the truth. Each and every one of them were trained killers, the women as well as the men. There was not a person inside the building who wouldn't kill a white or even a black person if Kenyatta so ordered it. They were all assassins, trained in the art of death.

Even the tall, attractive black woman who sat at his elbow could murder women or children if the need arose. Kenyatta had trained his small band of disciples so well that there was no feeling of guilt over an act of violence, no matter how brutal it might be. Whatever they did was justified as an application of justice—black justice. It was the only kind of justice that held any significant meaning to any of them. That white justice was a mockery could be seen openly every day in the court-rooms—used for the rich and forced on the poor.

"Red has gone to the farm," Kenyatta continued. Everybody was listening quietly to what he had to say. "I sent him and his lady on out with another couple. They took most of the guns with them, so we won't have to worry about transporting our weapons. I'm not sure, but the police may have been watching the place. When I say I'm not sure, I mean I don't have any idea why they would bother to go through the trouble of watching us.

We ain't doing nothing." His words brought laughter from his listeners.

Slowly, like a well-trained actor, Kenyatta raised his hand for silence. "I don't want to get into it real deep right now, but we got what we been waitin' for. I got the names of some of the biggest honkies in the fuckin' city. I'm talkin' about the motherfuckin' honkies who have been living out in Grosse Pointe, while selling dope down in the center city. Of course they don't have to come down here and sell it themselves, 'cause they got a good head nigger who goes by the name of Kingfisher. But once we knock Kingfisher's ass off, they goin' have mighty big trouble findin' another good nigger like him!"

There was a roar like the sea makes when it's beginning an angry storm. The storm was brewing right there in that small apartment. It had started to brew many years ago, before many of the dedicated young blacks were even born.

Zeke, the tall, light-brown-complexioned man who had been in on the holdup with Red, spoke up. "It's damn sure time, Ken," he stated, using the short nickname that only a few of Kenyatta's closest friends ever used.

There was the sound of the rear doorbell ringing. Instantly the people in the apartment became silent, each wondering who would be using the alley entrance. To get up the rear steps, a person had to come through the alley, then walk through a trash-littered garage, which led into the small enclosure that was the backyard. After getting to the yard, they could only come up on the rear porch and ring the back doorbell. The stairway that led upstairs was enclosed, so that somebody had to go down the back steps to unlock the door.

The people waited quietly to see who was coming up. Betty moved uneasily on her perch as the newcomer approached. As the man entered, everybody there recognized him. He was the kind of person who would be recognized in a crowd. His arrival caused a different kind of reaction in each person there, but the women reacted the most. Betty was not the only woman who moved back in fear.

The man wore a long black coat that was wrapped around him like a cloak, covering a tall, very spare body. Beneath the rounded dome of a closely shaved skull, large black eyes peered from either side of a jutting, beak-like nose. The mouth below was sunken, the lips puckered, and the chin had a sharp upward hook. With one dark brown hand the man caressed the bony line of his jaw, staring coldly around at the people in the room. Under the probing of those lusterless black eyes, each person either waved at him feebly or glanced away as if they hadn't noticed his searching stare. The atmosphere in the room changed. It was as if something unclean, something foul with slime, had crept amongst them.

Kenyatta seemed as if he was the only person in the room who hadn't noticed the change.

"What's happenin', Creeper?" he asked, as Creeper stopped in front of him.

Betty quickly got up from her perch on the side of the chair and walked back towards the kitchen. "I think I'll get a drink. You want one, daddy?" she asked over her shoulder.

"Naw, baby, I don't want anything, but Creeper might care for a drink." He glanced up at the man. As their gaze met, Kenyatta experienced a shrinking inner horror. This man was something he did not and could not understand. He was a man who was totally alien to his own world. The Creeper was one of the oldest members of his organization. He wasn't dedicated to any cause except Kenyatta, and only because Kenyatta had saved his life. He had been shot and wounded by the police, trying to find a hiding place in an alley, when Kenyatta had found him and taken him home, cared for his wound, then gave him a place to live. For that help, the tall black man called "the Creeper" had become like a shadow to Kenyatta.

"Well, what will it be, Creeper?" Betty asked, not trying to hide the dislike in her voice.

"Did I ask for anything?" Creeper replied, then turned his back on her as if she wasn't there. For some strange reason, out of all the people in Kenyatta's organization, Betty was the only one that Creeper really hated. Even he couldn't understand the intensity of his hatred for the woman. He blamed her for coming between him and Kenyatta, but it went deeper than that. He had never cared for another human being in his life. Then Kenyatta had come to his rescue. It was not just the help either, it was the way the other man treated him— like a man. Kenyatta didn't turn away from him in horror because of his looks. He'd been aware for years of his looks since he'd been a child, when kids had started calling him "the Creeper" because of the similarity of his features to those of the man who played the Creeper in the movies. In time, he'd come to accept it, not caring one way or another what they called him. He was a man who lived alone, until he met Kenyatta.

The man stood over Kenyatta until Kenyatta grew uneasy. "Well, what is it, brother? You seem to have something on your mind but you ain't saying nothing."

For an answer, Creeper let his eyes roam over the other people in the room. "You know me better than to think I'd say anything in front of them," he replied, loud enough for everybody to hear. "The first time one of these niggers gets uptight, they goin' blow this whole fuckin' thing up in your face, Kenyatta, you just wait and see."

Before Kenyatta could give an answer to that, Creeper let his coat slip open. "I took care of that little thing you asked me to handle for you," he stated harshly, not bothering to rebutton his coat.

For a minute Kenyatta couldn't think. The man standing in front of him was covered with blood. *What was the man talking about,* Kenyatta asked himself. He remembered asking the man to check up on Kingfisher's right-hand man, but other than that, he couldn't remember asking him to take care of anything.

Kenyatta rose from his chair in one smooth motion and beckoned with his head. "Come on," he said, leading the way towards the bedroom. He wanted to get to the bottom of this, and the sooner the better. Something had happened, and whatever it was, blood had been spilled.

Across town in his penthouse apartment, the Kingfisher moved around like a man struck down by an unknown force. The information that had just come to him was so shocking that he couldn't believe it. The Kingfisher was used to death but not when it was an act of gross mutilation so close to home.

As Kingfisher paced back and forth in his penthouse apartment, he kept murmuring to himself. "Too close, too fuckin' close to home . . . , if they can knock off my right-hand man." He shook his head, unnerved to his very roots by this murderous act.

8

——

AFTER THE BRUTAL DEATHS of Kenyatta's people by Kingfisher's hit men, Kenyatta had called
one person in and given him one assignment:
find out which ones were responsible, then handle it if you can. It hadn't taken the man that long
to find out who had given the order, and when he
reported back that it was the Kingfisher, he was
then given another order. If you can't get the big
fish, get the next biggest fish in the pond. Even
that order proved quite hard to do. The next biggest
fish was Kingfisher's right-hand man, Sam. Sam was
as hard to reach as the Kingfisher—almost.

It took a while for the Creeper to find the weak
link. He had the uncanny ability of being able to
pry into things that ordinary men would have
long given up on. The Creeper believed that every

man had a weakness, somewhere; all you had to
do was search for it, and eventually it would come
to light.

In the case of the Kingfisher's right-hand man
and trusted personal bodyguard, Sam, the truth
wasn't too hard to dig up. Once the Creeper found
out that Sam had a wife, two girls, and a four-year-
old boy, it was just a matter of time. The man who
had helped order the death of four members of
Kenyatta's organization would eventually show
up at his home. Only the Creeper didn't have the
patience to wait until Sam decided to pay his wife
and kids a visit. He decided to hurry the matter
up. Having already been given his orders, he didn't
bother to check back with Kenyatta. He did to the
best of his ability just what had been asked of him.

Mary, the woman who had made the mistake of
bearing two children for Sam, knew nothing of
Sam's business. All she knew was that he made a
good living. He was the first black man she had
ever lived with who took care of her and her children so well that she never worried about money
problems. Whenever she needed money, she just
called Sam and explained to him what she needed
it for and how much. It didn't really matter that
she didn't have a marriage license; Sam took care
of her better than the man she had married earlier
in her life. That marriage hadn't lasted but two
years, and in those two years she caught more hell
than the average woman ran into in a lifetime. But

the marriage had been legal. She kept the proof of her first marriage locked up in an iron chest in the closet, but she didn't really need it. The two girls who belonged to Sam were more proof than any piece of paper could ever be.

Her two girls by Sam were both born out of wedlock but, as far as she was concerned, Sam was her husband even though they had never gone before a preacher. He was good to all of his children. Whenever he bought something for the girls, he made sure he brought the boy something too. The girls, one three and the other fifteen months, were treated like small dolls by their father whenever he had the time to be around them. Most of the time he wasn't home, but he made sure they never wanted for anything. It was one of the few joys Sam really got out of life, buying things for the kids—things that he wasn't able to have when he was a child because of money problems.

The small family lived happily in this manner until the day that Mary saw a strange man bringing her son David home. The man was monstrous and ugly. Mary wondered how the preschool could allow such a person to work for them, but at once she regretted her thoughts. Even this human being had to live. It was for sure he hadn't made himself, so who was she to complain about his looks. Overwhelmed by pity, she opened her door wide, allowing the man who clutched her struggling son to enter.

"What did he do at school?" she managed to ask as they entered the house. "Do you have to hold him so roughly?" she inquired, as David tried to twist out of the vicious hold the man had on his arm. Tears rolled from David's eyes, even after the man released him. The man glanced around the house.

He noticed the expensive carpet on the floor and the dark brown wall-to-wall fabric that matched the golden colored furnishings. The couch and matching chair, the marble coffee table, the solid marble end tables, all gave an idea of the good life that was being lived here.

"Oh, Sam don't do too bad for himself, do he?" the man inquired. His voice was low and carried a sharp note in it.

At the mention of Sam, Mary's heart seemed to freeze. She realized at once this wasn't something her son had done at school. The man had used David as an excuse to get inside the house. *Oh, my God,* she thought to herself. Suddenly the baby girl started crying in her playpen, which was kept right in the front room.

As she started to go to the child, she said, "There must be some mistake somewhere. This Sam you're talking about, he doesn't live here."

She had to pass between the man and the coffee table to reach the child. He reached out and pushed her back.

"If I were you, honey child," Creeper said

coldly, "I wouldn't worry too much about that child crying."

"Well, you don't happen to be me!" Mary yelled at him as she attempted to jerk her arm free.

What happened then seemed more like a dream to her than reality. It had been so long since someone had put their hands on her. His hand came up slowly, or so it seemed to Mary, and he slapped her across the face twice.

"Now, honey child," he began in that same singsong voice, "I want you to cooperate with me." Seeing the defiant look come into her eyes, he grinned. "This is no joke, girl. If you love your kids, you will do just what I ask of you."

He shoved her down on the couch, causing her housecoat to fly up, but she paid small heed to that. If rape was all the man wanted, she was willing if only he'd get it over with and leave—leave just like he came, without really harming anyone. But in the back of her mind she knew it wouldn't be that simple. This man wasn't interested in fucking her. She could sense something monstrous and grotesque about him, an evil that she couldn't completely grasp.

Shuddering with repugnance she managed to ask, "What is it you want?"

"Why, child, I've already told you. Sam. I want the big shot, Sam the man." His laughter came then, cold, chilling, frightening.

She tried again. "Please, I've already told. . . ."

The lie froze in her throat. The man had produced a straight razor from his pocket and opened it quickly.

"That's right, child," he said in that same funny tone. "I'm not here to play games. Now, if you keep lying, I'm going to cut that boy's throat right in front of you."

Could this be true? Could it really be happening?

She wanted to pinch herself to see if she was asleep. Mary tried to close and reopen her eyes. It was just too much to believe. The man couldn't possibly be so bloodthirsty as to kill her son. The very thought of it was too much for her mind to accept.

"Please!" She made a small feeble gesture with her hand, trying to express what she couldn't find the words to say. She still couldn't believe that the man would hurt her child. "Listen, I don't have any way to reach Sam. He calls me."

The words were hardly out of her mouth before the man went into action. He didn't waste any time. It was as if he were butchering a cow. He snatched the small boy to him and drew the sharp razor across the boy's throat before she realized what had happened. The quick flow of blood that came from the wound brought her to her senses. The man pushed the boy away and the small child fell onto the floor.

An animal cry of pain came from the woman then, as she stumbled down beside the child. There was nothing she could do. As she clutched the child to her, his life's blood ran out in her lap. From the floor she glared up at the Creeper, shocked almost out of her mind.

"One down and two to go," he said in a quiet voice as he moved over towards the little girl in the playpen. She was still a toddler. She stood there looking up at the man with her arms outstretched for him to pick her up.

Something deep down inside Mary warned her that her anguish would have to be controlled if she wanted to save the rest of her family. "Please, no more," she cried, "I'll call him." With those words she started to weep. The outburst was not convulsive but sheer grief. A grief that would never find that gratifying relief in tears.

"Mommie, Mommie," the dark-haired three-year-old cried, "what's wrong, Mommie?"

Mary pulled the child to her, her arms gripping the child tightly. Mary was a tall woman in her late twenties. Built heavy from delivering babies, she now had the body of a woman—a big woman. Large arms that spoke of strength—she was a woman who could work in the fields beside her man if it was ever necessary.

The little child with the pigtails running down each side of her head began to cry. She wanted the tall man beside her to reach down and pick her up.

Impatiently, the Creeper reached down and rubbed the child's head. In his other hand he held the bloody razor. Mary glanced up from where she was kneeling, her heart almost stopping.

"Please," she begged, "I'll call, I'll call." Her hands groped wildly for the phone. "Get Mommie the phone," she said to the small child beside her. The little girl ran off at once, pulling the telephone off the end table and dragging it back toward her crying mother. Tears continued to run down Mary's cheeks, but no sound came out. She knew the little boy she held in her lap was gone. Now the only thing she could hope for was to save her girls. Sam, big, strong Sam—he would know how to handle this madman! The thought flashed through her mind as she tried to remember the number he had given her to call in case of an emergency. Desperately she dialed the number, only to find out that she had called the wrong one. She stopped and tried to get her mind right. She had to think right. She fought down the desire to throw herself against the madman. It would be useless. No matter how strong she was, there was something about the man that spoke of pure danger. Even as fear-ridden as she was, she wondered if Sam would be able to do anything with him. She couldn't see this skinny man being able to contain all that strength. No, Sam would handle him when he got here.

Apprehension filled her very soul as she watched the man stroke her child's head. "Please, leave the baby alone," she managed to say. "I'm making your call for you, so just leave my child alone."

The man's hand stopped in mid-air. "Okay, dear," he said softly, as he turned away from the playpen. "Just get the call through."

Vaguely she heard another voice on the other end of the phone. "Sam," she blurted out, "I've got to speak to Sam!" It took a few seconds, then she heard his strong voice on the line. She blurted out something about one of the children being hurt, then begged him to come home at once so that he could rush the child to the hospital.

The message got across to Sam. He made a hurried excuse to Kingfisher and left.

If there was one thing Sam didn't want, it was one of his hood friends ever coming in contact with his family. For some reason, he believed if he kept his friends away there would never be any problem. None of the dirt that he dealt in would rub off. He would have been hard pressed to explain it himself if asked, but either way he made sure none of his friends ever visited him while he was staying with Mary.

For a brief moment after Sam left, Kingfisher was undecided on whether or not he should have some of the boys follow him. But just as quickly as the notion came into his head, he dismissed it. Sam was his most trusted man, and if he couldn't trust Sam, who the hell could he trust? Later he was to regret having made that decision, for if he had followed through with it, he might have been able to put an end to his troubles right then and there.

It took Sam less than thirty minutes to reach his beautiful red-brick home in Conant Gardens, a black neighborhood that only the blacks with above-average incomes could buy into. He pulled into the driveway. As he jumped out and ran for the front door, he was surprised that Mary hadn't come out to meet him. The woman was able to carry the child just as well as he was, and if it was as serious as she said, she would have been waiting for him at the door.

As he ran across the well-kept lawn he noticed the front door was cracked halfway open. He jumped up on the porch and didn't stop until he had burst through the front door. Then he stopped abruptly. At first he couldn't believe his eyes. His mind didn't want to accept what he saw. He wiped his eyes with the back of his hand, only to find the sight still there when he reopened them. The first thing that came to his sight was his baby daughter, her pen pushed in front of the front door so that whoever entered would have to walk around it to get into the front room. The small child lay out on the clean mattress, clean except for the dried blood around the slit in her neck. Other than that, it was as if the little girl was sleeping.

Even as he stumbled over to her pen, his mind told him that it had been done with a razor. He started to reach down and pick up the child, but again his mind informed him that it was a useless action; the baby was dead. Tears blinded him as he staggered around the pen.

Then he saw Mary. She was tied to the end of the marble coffee table. Her throat was cut, too, and she had cuts across her face as if she had tried to fight until the end. But the dead children lying around the room showed how useless it had been. His three-year-old girl was lying close to her mother, only her throat was not cut. The madman had deviated. Instead of the razor, he had strangled the little girl with her own pigtails.

Sam dropped on his knees beside the three-year-old, praying that there still might be life in the small body. His brain screamed over and over again, *Who could be responsible for such a monstrous act?* This wasn't the work of a sane mind. Whoever had committed these insane acts had more than just enjoyed them. He must have received a certain macabre fascination from such grotesque butchery. To be able to kill an adult was one thing; to kill children was another. But to be able to butcher a baby was yet another kind of murdering beast, one who needed to be destroyed at once.

For the moment though, Sam was too stricken even to think of revenge. He wanted to make whoever did this pay, but his mind was too shocked. Could this be some kind of payback for the killing Kingfisher had ordered? It was hard for him to reason that out. He thought he was dealing with men, and even though he knew they were violent men, it had never occurred to him that they were insane, and that was the only explanation he could

come up with for whoever had done this grue-
some work.

Then suddenly he heard it. It was low at first,
but as he listened it grew. The low laughter began
almost below the range of his hearing, then it
picked up until he could pinpoint the source. He
turned toward the sound. He hadn't tried to visu-
alize what the person might have looked like, but
now as he turned and saw the bloody human ap-
parition standing behind the full-length window
curtains, he knew at once that this debased human
was responsible for the destruction of everything
he loved in this life. As he stared at the human
riffraff, an almost imperceptible hatred increased
inside his brain until it was a full-blown desire to
destroy this thing.

The sound that came from the man's mouth
didn't even seem human; he was enjoying every
moment of this. He loved the sight of the grief that
had overcome the big heavyset man. It seemed to
bring him joy to watch the expressions that flashed
across Sam's face.

Sam wanted to kill and destroy, and yet he also
wanted to know. "Why, man? Why the kids?" he
asked as he moved slowly across the room, unaware that he had even taken a step. The same
question kept coming from him as he stalked the
grinning Creeper, who watched him approach
with a twisted smile on his face.

The enveloping blackness that invaded Sam's

mind stopped him from thinking, or even reasoning. All he could do was move as if he were some kind of automaton—a machine with but one thought. There could be no other reason for him to continue to exist. To destroy, that was the only thought in his mind now. He had to destroy this creature that had so destroyed his life. Whatever else he had to do in life was gone from his thoughts. There wasn't anything left for him to do. His hands turned into huge claws. He didn't make a fist, but held his hands out and continued to move slowly toward the man across the living room. He didn't even notice the thirty-eight automatic with the long silencer that the man now held out in front of him.

The blood on the man's clothes only helped to drive Sam mad. The nearer he got, the more he could smell the stench of death that was on the man. The blood represented his family, his loved ones. The word still came from him as he neared his goal. "Why, why, why?"

The Creeper took his time and concentrated on the huge man's chest. The first shot didn't even seem to hit Sam as he continued his slow stalking of the murderer. There was no squeamishness about the Creeper though. He only grinned and pulled the trigger again. The silencer took care of all the noise. The second bullet that struck Sam sort of slowed him down, but he continued on after hesitating for a second. The third shot went unheeded, and so did the fourth. Now sweat broke out on the Creeper's forehead as he raised the gun a little higher and pulled the trigger. This shot blew the left eye out of Sam's face. He didn't resemble anything human anymore. But a strength derived from his hatred of what stood in front of him kept him on his feet.

The Creeper started to back up but had nowhere to go. The picture window had him blocked in. The only way out was past the stalking Sam, who continued to move, if ever so slowly, toward the killer. With one shot left in his gun, the Creeper took dead aim. Nothing under the sun could stand up to six well-placed shots. Nothing human, anyway.

Now Sam was less than two feet away. He raised his arms to put his hands around the frail neck that was in front of him. He had forgotten why he even wanted to kill this thing in front of him. He was past that form of thinking. He was moving only through of some inner strength that knew what stood in front of him must be destroyed. He stretched his arms out, but the Creeper wasn't a weak man either. Being evil, he thrived on evil. He was also a brave man, and he was a killer. He was a man who didn't need the strength of other men to give him courage. He feared nothing mortal.

Even as Sam approached, even though his heart skipped a beat, he kept the sneer on his face and kept complete confidence in his gun. He waited until the outstretched fingers almost touched his face before using his last bullet. This time he aimed right at the center of the forehead. Nothing human could survive a shot at such close range. The bullet tore half of Sam's head off. The man crumpled up as if he was a rag doll at the feet of the Creeper.

9

THE DETROIT POLICE DEPARTMENT was caught completely by surprise. The city seemed to burst wide open in a blood bath. They had been used to murder in the surrounding black ghettos, but now, in the last two weeks, three white gangsters, known to have been big men in the organization, had been found dead. The similarity of some of the murders to those that they had found out in Conant Gardens was too close to ignore. Nobody but an insane person killed with a straight razor, and two of the white gangsters had been found with their throats cut. One of them had been found with his wife dead beside him, and she had been killed the same way. There had to be a tie-in somewhere. At least that was what Captain Davidson believed, and this he passed on to his men at a meeting inside his office.

The afternoon sun blazed through his open window. Benson and Ryan loosened their collars, but Detectives Steward and Nelson didn't notice the heat. Their problem was the tough old captain who didn't want to hear any excuses. There had been too many deaths lately. Something would have to be done or somebody would be replaced, and it could be the captain from the way things were going. The captain paced up and down his office, wearing a groove in the dirty, three-colored rug on the floor. It had been there so long that there was a pale outline of where the captain and his predecessor had paced back and forth. Detectives Benson and Ryan watched him calmly. Suddenly he stopped and sat on the edge of his beaten-up desk.

"I don't care for no excuses," he began. "I've had enough of them to last a lifetime. This shit has got to come to an end. This kind of murdering just won't be tolerated by the newspapers, and when the newspapers start playing up something like this, heads begin to roll." He held his hand up for silence. "Now, I don't want to replace any of you guys, 'cause I know you're doing your best, but I'll have to replace somebody just to prove I'm trying. Now, do you see where I'm at?"

He stared around at the four men, his eyes steel gray points peering out over the large horn-rimmed glasses he wore. "I like my job. I mean to keep it. So if something don't come up soon, some of you guys had better dust off those old blue uniforms you used to wear when you were in the ranks."

Suddenly Captain Davidson snapped his fingers in the direction of Detective Steward. The young, blond detective glanced down at the worn rug. "And you," the captain began again, "I asked you two weeks ago to get in touch with Ryan and Benson here about that first murder, but oh, no, not you. You're too fuckin' smart. What did you tell me? Wasn't no spade behind that hit. It had to be organization crap. It was too big for a spade. Wasn't that your opinion?"

The younger man looked away, not wanting Benson to see his eyes and not wanting the captain to see through him. He still couldn't believe that blacks were behind it, unless it was a big, important black gangster, and there really wasn't but one that big in the city.

Steward glanced over at his partner, Nelson, then spoke what was on his mind. "Captain, it's not but one black man in this city big enough to even think about making a hit on these guys, and that's the one they call the Kingfisher."

The roar the captain let out could be heard throughout the building. "Kingfisher, my ass! He's in the same fuckin' pot that all the big shits uptown are in. Those were his men that got knocked off first. Those happened to be his pushers that got knocked off last week. But I forgot. You're too big of a guy to keep up with the little people that get killed in the ghettos. And since you didn't, let me clue you in. That pusher killed last week was one of the Kingfisher's men."

Steward shrugged, then speculated quietly, "Maybe they got a gang war going on? I mean, who else would even have the names of these big wheels? I just can't picture some small hood down in the ghetto coming up with the information he'd need to reach these guys."

For a minute, as Benson watched, he thought the captain was about to have a heart attack. The man turned red in the face, then he seemed to have trouble breathing. He leaned over the desk, trying to catch his breath, and when he straightened up, sparks flew from his eyes.

"Boy," the captain roared, "I don't give a fuck what you can't picture, do you understand that? I want you and your partner to get off your fuckin' asses and do what I say. When I say get in touch with Ryan and Benson and compare notes, I mean just that."

Nobody bothered to speak. They all just stared at the captain. All of them had seen him in his moods before, but nothing like this. He was really upset, which just went to show them how important it must be for them to solve the spree of crimes.

The last thing Benson wanted was to have to work alongside the two young officers whom he disliked, but it looked as if he wouldn't have any choice in the matter. Things had gone too far; there had to be an end to them.

* * *

At the same time that they were having their discussion at police headquarters, another meeting was going on at the penthouse that belonged to Kingfisher.

Kingfisher paced his front room just as the captain paced his tiny office, only the Kingfisher was scared—not frightened from fear of losing a job but frightened for his life. It was getting too close for comfort. He didn't need anybody to spell it out for him. He knew beyond a shadow of a doubt that he was on the death list. He glared at his henchmen as he paced past them.

"I'm telling you guys for the last time," he swore angrily, "that I don't want nobody . . . , and I mean just that, nobody . . . , who hasn't been here before to get into this apartment. If somebody tries, I want that man or woman held, searched, and make damn sure they don't have no kind of weapon on them. But when I say don't let nobody back here to these apartments, I mean just that. I don't even want a goddamn fly coming in. You guys want me to write that out for you, or do you understand?"

Kingfisher stared from one face to another, then spoke to a lean man standing near the black grand piano. "Big-Time, what's been happenin' on that matter I sent you to? Did you get in touch with the fuckin' creeps?" Before Big-Time could answer any of the questions, Kingfisher began again. "These punks are the reason behind every fuckin' thing going on. I know it, I feel it here." He placed his hand over his heart. "We didn't have no trouble until this punk Kenyatta comes along talkin' about you can't sell no more drugs in the ghetto. Who the fuck does he think he is?"

Finally Big-Time spoke up. "I been going by this joint they got over on the north end, you know, but the place is damn near deserted. I finally caught a dame there and gave her the message, you know, and she says to check back with her the next day. So when I go there, here the bitch is already waiting for me."

He slowed down, to make sure the Kingfisher was listening, then continued. "Well, the dame asked me right off, as soon as I entered the joint, if you done quit pushing dope inside the city. I hesitated for a minute on that one, King, 'cause I didn't know what to say. But before I could even lie, the broad speaks up again. She says they know fuckin' damn well you ain't, but she says to tell you that Kenyatta says he's taking care of your white friends right now and he'll see to it personally that somebody checks you out 'cause you're the one who's really putting that shit in the ghetto."

Before he finished talking, Big-Time had removed a hankie from his center pocket and wiped his brow. He didn't like the message any better than his boss, and it was obvious that the Kingfisher didn't like it at all.

It was as if somebody had hit the Kingfisher in

the stomach with a fist. The man stood in the middle of the floor blowing like a fish out of water. "She said that? The part about knockin' off my white friends?"

As the Kingfisher waited for Big-Time to answer, he stared at the man's face, reading whether or not Big-Time was lying. Then he did something that took all his men by surprise: he turned around and counted them. When he finished, he said, "Let's go. I want to talk to this bitch myself."

Eight men got up to leave. "Who we goin' leave to watch the pad?" Big-Time asked when they reached the door.

The Kingfisher stared around in surprise. "Is this all the help I got?" he asked sharply. "Two of you guys stay. That still leaves seven of us, counting myself."

It was left up to Big-Time to appoint two men to stay and watch the place. "Make sure," he ordered sharply, more for his boss' benefit than for the men, "to check on every fuckin' thing that comes near the place. We won't be gone but a short time."

"Should we take both cars?" Big-Time inquired as they reached the downstairs floor. The elevator deposited them in the plush lobby. As they got out, one of Kingfisher's men stuck a key into the lock of the elevator so that nobody would use it until they came back. If the apartment caught on fire, the few people up there would have to use the escape route, taking the stairway, which was closed by a heavy iron door. Other than that, there was no way into the penthouse.

Before the group of men left the plush lobby, a young bellboy made his way to the pay phone. He dialed quickly and spoke quietly into the telephone. He hung up and went back to his work.

"Just bring around the Caddy," Kingfisher ordered before leaving the lobby. With one hand, Big-Time made a sign to the chauffeur, who stayed downstairs for just such an occasion. The man rushed outside so that, by the time the rest of the party was reaching the street, the long Cadillac was pulling up in front of the apartment building.

All three of the cars were kept parked outside under the supervision of the man who stayed in the lobby. It was his job to make sure none of the cars were ever tampered with. He was also one of the drivers. Generally, they took along two cars. Kingfisher didn't like to be crowded. But today he didn't seem to mind the thought of all seven men squeezing into the car.

As the men walked towards the long car, a black Ford turned the corner swiftly and bore down on the group of men. It didn't take a man with a lot of imagination to know what was going on. Even as the car hurled toward them, they could see the windows rolling down and the snouts of the short-barreled guns sticking out of the windows.

The Kingfisher let out a high-pitched scream

that would have done a woman justice. Then the tall, tan-complexioned man began to scramble toward the waiting car. He had to shove some of his bodyguards out of the way, but he managed to throw himself through the front door of the waiting Cadillac before the Ford reached them. Some of his gunmen, made out of better stuff, held their ground, pulling guns from under their coats. But the pistols were no match for the bursts from the submachine guns as the car roared past. All the bullets that struck the Cadillac bounced off because the car was bulletproof. But the men standing on the sidewalk weren't. They fell as if someone had cut them down with a mowing machine.

As the Kingfisher huddled down on the floor of his car, he could feel a weight on his back. He glanced up and saw the frightened face of Big-Time.

"They're gone," the driver, Jack, stated as coldly as he could. He glanced over his shoulder at the men lying on the sidewalk, then glanced down at the two big men lying on the floor. He gritted his teeth. "They knocked off at least three of the boys," he said, his voice not revealing the contempt he felt for both of the men who were on the floor. He could understand running for your life, but he had seen them both push men out of the way who were only trying to get their guns out so that they could defend the two cowards who ran so quickly.

"You still want to make that trip?" Big-Time asked from where he lay huddled on the floor.

Jack had to grin when Kingfisher answered sharply, "The only thing I want, nigger, is for you to get your big ass off of me so I can get the hell out of this goddamn car and get back into the apartment. We goin' have to think on this shit a little more deeper."

Kingfisher climbed out of the car, glancing both ways to make sure there was no chance of his getting caught in the open as he made his dash for the doorway. He didn't bother to pay any attention to his men, whose bodies lay sprawled out on the sidewalk. He had only one thought, and that was to get to the protection of his penthouse, which now had become for him a prison.

10

THE DETECTIVES ARRIVED and the Kingfisher was ready for them. His white lawyer, Mr. Booth, was there to answer all the questions for him. He had only to lie back on his couch and nod his head.

Benson stood on the sidelines and watched. So this was the big man he had heard so much about. *The sonofabitch is so scared he's damn near shittin' in his pants,* the detective reflected coldly.

"So, you say," Nelson asked for what seemed like the twentieth time, "that you saw this car come hurdling around the corner and you knew at once it had hit men in it? Now, you don't really expect us to believe this crap that you didn't recognize any of these so-called hit men, do you?"

The Kingfisher just shrugged his shoulders. "I don't give a flying fuck what you believe," he stated harshly. "I done told you what happened, what I saw, now you can take it from there."

Nelson shrugged his shoulders. He wasn't used to black men talking that way to him. "We could take you downtown, you know. Then maybe you'd feel like cooperating with us."

Benson had to glance away to keep the smile from coming to his lips, but he didn't look away fast enough. His partner, Ryan, recognized the look, and hid his own smile. Taking the Kingfisher downtown on some bullshit would be like sticking your head in a lion's mouth to see if he had a toothache.

Ryan walked over to his partner. "What do you think about all this shit?" he asked seriously.

Benson shrugged. "If the guy really knew anything, he'd talk. Three of his boys got knocked off, one was hurt seriously enough to go to the hospital, plus he's scared so bad he's damn near ready to shit on himself every time somebody comes through that door. He'd talk, all right. You can bet on it."

Ryan nodded. "That's the same way I got it figured, but I think he knows something. I don't know what it is, but he's got a damn good idea who's trying to knock him off."

"We'll see," Benson said as he walked over toward the man on the couch. For some reason, he derived a joyous warmth from seeing the fear in the man. This was the bastard who supplied the whole fuckin' city with dope, and yet none of them could touch him. In fact, they had to handle him with kid gloves, or they would have their asses in a sling by the next day.

It was easy to see from the frowns on Nelson's and Steward's faces that they didn't like the idea of the older detective moving in while they were interrogating the gangster.

"When you finish talking with these boys, King, I'd like to have a private little conversation with you if it's possible," Benson inquired quietly.

The Kingfisher didn't waste any time. He just got up off the couch, ignoring the two young detectives who had been talking to him. "Let's step back in my bedroom. Maybe we can find some kind of privacy there," he said after tossing a look at his lawyer.

Benson shook his head. "It's not necessary for him to come along, but if you want him, it's up to you," Benson said softly.

Before opening the door that led into the bedroom, the Kingfisher stopped and stared silently at the officer. He waved his lawyer off. Neither man spoke until after the door was closed. Benson glanced around the well-furnished bedroom. Everything inside it was expensive. The king-sized bed had a deep red bedspread on it and the carpet on the floor was black, mixed with a dark red strain that matched the rest of the room.

"I might as well come straight to the point," Benson began. "I believe you and I both know who's responsible for this shit. I know you don't want any kind of gang war, but this young bastard I'm thinking about wouldn't care one way or the other." It was a shot in the dark for Benson. He didn't know for sure who was behind the killings.

"You're goddamn right," Kingfisher roared. "That fuckin' Kenyatta ain't got enough sense to pour pee out of a boot!"

So there it was, Benson reflected. After all was said and done, it really was Kenyatta behind it all. "How the hell would a guy like Kenyatta go about gettin' the kind of information he'd need to knock off some of these dagos he's hit?" Benson inquired. "I mean, I can understand him gettin' a fix on you but not on some of them white boys."

Kingfisher tossed his hands in the air. 'That's the goddamn problem right there. For a minute some of the big guys thought I was responsible for it, but he's made a hit on one guy that I didn't know shit about." Kingfisher fell silent for a minute, then continued. "After the big boys stopped and put their thinking caps on, they realized that it wouldn't make sense for me to be in on this kind of shit. Why? I mean, I'd have everything to lose and nothing to gain." The Kingfisher shook his head. "Naw, they realize it couldn't be me. I've told them everything I know about this creep, too."

As the Kingfisher talked, Benson realized that the man was trying to sell the idea to himself that the big boys really believed him when he said he didn't have anything to do with it. He must be in

the middle of it, Benson reasoned as he watched
the bigtime dope pusher try to make sense out of
what was happening.

The Kingfisher continued to talk. "Them was
black dudes that tried to make that hit on us
today; there ain't no doubt about that. I got a good
peep at them, even if I can't pick none of them
out of a lineup." The man was really talking to
himself, trying to figure out what was happening
to the world he lived in.

"These punks came out of nowhere, it seemed,"
he continued. "It was like something out of the
roaring twenties. I mean, guys don't go in for this
kind of shit no more. It don't pay off. It hurts
where it shouldn't, in the pocketbook!"

Benson didn't cut him off. He just let the big
man talk. This was the best information he had
come up with yet.

"The only problem is where could this punk
have gotten the information he's got? If I knew
the answer to that one, I'd be able to bust this shit
wide open."

All at once Benson changed the conversation.
"Where do you suppose a guy like that could come
up with the weapons he's gettin', man? I know you
could get your hands on a chopper or two, but for
the average nigger in the ghetto, buying a submachine gun is like trying to catch a ride to the
moon."

Benson watched his face as he asked the question. He knew he was giving out something, but

he honestly didn't know where Kenyatta was coming up with the heavy guns.

All at once Kingfisher snapped his fingers. "It ain't many places, I can tell you. Offhand, I couldn't come up with but two or three people. . . ." Suddenly he stopped talking and a light came into his eyes. He smiled coldly and stood up from the edge of the bed. "Our interview is over with, copper. I got business to take care of," he said and opened the bedroom door.

Kingfisher didn't even bother to look back to see if the detective was following him. He walked straight over to his lawyer and spoke in a voice that could be heard all over the room. "How long have we got to put up with this shit? Can't you get rid of some of these people? I got business to take care of."

Benson didn't even bother to wait to see how the little fat lawyer would go about trying to get rid of the policemen crowding the apartment. He went to his partner and whispered something in his ear. Both men left immediately.

Neither man bothered to speak until they reached the sidewalk. "I think that's the key, Ryan," Benson said to his partner as they hurried toward the car. "When I mentioned the gun connect, he almost jumped out of his skin. It dawned on him then, just as it did me. The person supplying the information is the same one Kenyatta gets his guns from. It can't be any different."

Ryan got behind the steering wheel, listening

to his partner. "I don't know why we didn't see it before. Now all we got to do is find out who the hell is big enough to supply the kind of guns Kenyatta is using and we got our man."

"We already got a damn good idea of who that is," Ryan stated as he pulled out into the traffic. He didn't bother to look at the surprised expression on his partner's face.

"Like hell you say!" Benson exploded. "If we knew that much, we'd have come down on these bastards long before now."

"Well, we can't prove it, but just stop and think. You ain't forgot the day we seen that fat bastard coming out of Kenyatta's place, have you? Well, we checked out the license number and that took us up into a dead end. But don't forget, we also checked out the ownership of the place and found out it was owned by a black man, so whoever fat boy was, I kind of think he was our man."

Ryan fell silent for a minute, then added, "You and I have been doing some piss-poor police work, Ben. We've had this clue and haven't taken advantage of it. Why? Because we weren't sure. But now, we've got to turn up every fuckin' thing."

Ryan watched his partner struggle with the dilemma.

"Okay, Ryan, what now? We didn't see the guy well enough to really recognize him in the mug books." Benson sat up straight and grinned from ear to ear like a kid. "But now that we know the bastard probably handles guns, all we got to do is check out the mug books for bigtime gunrunners, and the first sonofabitch that even resembles that fat bastard will have a hell of a lot of questions to answer."

Ryan picked up speed and cut in and out of the traffic. At last they had something they could put their teeth into. Something a little more solid than a hope or a hunch.

"What about our informers?" Ryan asked as he lit up a smoke. "You think one of them might be able to come up with something that might also help?"

Benson shook his head. "Naw, it's been too big for them so far, so why even think in that direction. I believe this should be our biggest break. If we get our hands on the man supplying the guns, we got him. I think we better hurry before Kingfisher puts the word out, too. The big boys ain't going to like the idea of someone giving out information on them like this. It's got three of them knocked off already, and no telling how many other names are still on that fuckin' list."

Ryan shook his head in agreement. "I'd sure like to get a look at that list. It would make our work a hell of a lot easier. If we could have gotten the Kingfisher to tell us a little more about who some of his friends are, it would have helped."

"It's easier to get help from hell," Benson answered shortly. "Kingfisher is scared to death, but not that scared."

As they neared the ramp leading to the freeway,

a car swerved in front of them, causing Ryan to slam on his brakes. "Damn!" Ryan cursed loudly as both men braced themselves for the sudden stop.

"That's one damn good theory, Ben, about that list. It makes sense, all right. In fact, it makes more sense than anything we've come up with yet."

Benson accepted the compliment quietly. He hoped that he was on the right path. Too many people had been killed.

Ryan cut into his thoughts sharply, bringing him back to reality. "Even with the death of the Kingfisher's right-hand man, we have to come to the conclusion that it ties in with the murders downtown." Before Benson could add his little bit, Ryan continued, speaking in that soft voice he used whenever he was thinking out loud. "The brutal killing of the children doesn't fit in with gangland killing though. Professional killers would never have butchered the children."

"Maybe the guy was trying to force information from the woman and he attempted to influence her by brutalizing the children." Benson made a small gesture with his hands, then dropped them back into his lap. As he continued to speak, his words came slowly, as if it hurt him to speak.

"Something like this, Ryan, tears me up. I've seen a lot of killings, but the way them kids were done up, it makes me sick to my stomach to even think about it."

The traffic on the freeway was moving swiftly

so it didn't take but minutes before Ryan reached his exit, the Jefferson Avenue ramp going west. He came off the freeway and made a right-hand turn.

"I was wondering," Benson began, "if we might have gotten better information from the Feds. A guy who sells guns on this scale might be somebody the FBI would be keepin' tabs on."

"Now you mention it!" Ryan roared. "You wait patiently until I get us back to police headquarters, then you drop this bombshell on me!" Even as he spoke, he drove past the garage where he ordinarily would have parked their car.

As they drove through the main part of downtown, Benson grinned to himself. He could tell his partner liked the idea, even though Ryan didn't come out and say it.

The traffic in the heart of town was congested, but Ryan moved in and out rather swiftly. He got a sharp glance from a policeman on a motorcycle as he got the jump on a crowded bus taking off from the red light from the inside lane.

When he reached Michigan Avenue, he had trouble trying to locate a parking spot. "Why don't you just put the bastard in a no-parking zone?" Benson inquired as they circled the block.

"Man," Benson began, "if I knew we were going to have to hitchhike all the way over to the Federal Building from our parking spot, I'd have called the dispatcher and had him send a squad car to drop us off."

"Like hell!" Ryan answered. "It's just another

one of your smart ideas coming eight hours too late, that's all."

On the second time around the block, Ryan saw a driver climbing into his car in front of the Federal Building in a no parking zone. Ryan grinned, pulling into the spot as soon as the driver pulled away from the curb.

"I didn't notice any ticket on his car," Ryan stated, backing up smoothly and parking. Benson got out first and waited on the sidewalk for his partner.

Ryan joined him. "I don't give a shit, Ben, what time it is when we finish, but whatever it is, I'm going to find me some place to eat. I ain't never seen a bastard like you. You just don't believe in eating!"

The men joked back and forth as they made their way into the building and caught the elevator up to the fifth floor. They made their inquiries, then showed their badges. A woman led them down the hall to an almost empty suite. There were two women working, one behind a huge typewriter that looked as if it had seen better days, while the other, a tall blonde, was sitting behind a rather dingy looking desk covered with papers. Both women glanced up when the threesome entered. The tall blonde got up from her desk and came to meet them before they could step behind the enclosure. "You gentlemen will have to wait here at the counter while I bring the mug books to you."

Both men shrugged and waited patiently until

she returned carrying three large books. "Well, since you fellows seem to be in good hands, I'll depart," the matronly-looking woman who had brought them to the mug files said.

Neither man glanced up from the books they had taken and laid out on the counter. The woman put the third book next to them and returned to her desk.

For the next hour, both men pored over the books until perspiration was running freely from their brows. The woman had come and gone with fresh books so many times that she became irritated when they called to her for more.

After another hour, Ryan snapped his finger down on a mug shot. "I couldn't swear on it, Ben, 'cause all I got was a side view of the bastard, but this could be him. Those fuckin' double chins of his were kind of hard to hide."

Benson glanced over his shoulder at the picture, then almost shoved his partner out of the way. He stared hard at the mug shot, while his agile mind went back to that day in front of Kenyatta's place.

The shrill voice of the blonde interrupted his concentration. "It's my lunchtime," she stated harshly. "You men will just have to come back later today if you don't have what you want now. We close this department at lunchtime."

Benson continued to study the mug shot in front of him, both men ignoring the woman standing there tapping her foot.

Benson finally ended his examination of the picture. He said only two words to his partner: "That's him."

The statement was brief, but there was no doubt in Ryan's mind about whether or not his partner was right or wrong. If Benson said that was their man, then that was the man they were going to run down.

As the woman reached over and tried to close the large book, Ryan coldly shoved her hand away. He read the name under the picture.

"You think we need a picture of the guy?" Ryan asked as Benson turned away from the counter.

Again his partner was brief and to the point. "Naw, it ain't necessary. I say we pick the fat punk up now."

"After we eat," Ryan said, and both men laughed as they started toward the door.

11

———

THE SPRAWLING ACREAGE of the farm was shown to its best when the sun was setting behind the wooded area at the end of the riding paths. The few horses that were kept on the farm were out in the small enclosure behind the huge white barn that contained most of the hay and grain fed to the livestock.

As Kenyatta glanced out of the upstairs bedroom window in the main farmhouse, he could see riders coming out of the wooded section and heading for the huge white barn. Scattered along their path were the many smaller cabins that surrounded the main building. As the horseback riders got closer, Kenyatta could make out his right-hand man, Ali, riding tall in the saddle. The man's name left a bitter taste in his mouth. Ali wanted all the rewards that went with big money, but he didn't want to do anything for it.

Kenyatta finished the cigarette he was smoking and glanced around for an ashtray. His mind wandered back to the conversation he had just had on the phone. His gun connect was finished. The fat honky was scared to death. The man hadn't been able to accept the killings Kenyatta's people had put on the big white dope pushers.

As Kenyatta thought about it, he smiled grimly. What had the man expected when he took their money for the goddamn information? Did he think Kenyatta was paying out that kind of bread just for kicks? Whatever the bastard thought, he had come out and told Kenyatta that the gun connect was finished.

Finished hell, Kenyatta reflected. If that fat bastard thought he was going to get out of it that easy, he had enough sense to make a jackass fly backward. No way, no fuckin' way in the world was Kenyatta going to allow Angelo's fat ass to get away with his money and the knowledge the man possessed. He was the only one who had the slightest idea of who was behind the hits. If he decided to sell that information, he wouldn't have any trouble finding buyers.

Betty opened the bedroom door and came in carrying a small silver tray with two drinks on it. "Here, honey, I thought you might like something cool."

As he took the offered drink, he smiled down

at the tall, attractive black woman. There was something about the way she carried herself—the way she held her head high in a lofty manner. There was the mark of nobility about her. Each time she took a step, her long red gown would open up, revealing a beautiful black leg. Her hair was done up in a huge natural, and her ears were adorned with large African earrings.

"I want you to get on the phone and start calling until you reach the Creeper for me. It's very important that I talk to him at once," Kenyatta ordered as he took the drink, then turned away from the beautiful woman. His mind was on other things at the moment, yet if he kept looking at her, he knew he would end up postponing something while he took a quick roll in the hay.

She seemed to read his mind. "I was hopin', daddy, that you might find time to take care of a little bit of your homework. It's been neglected lately, for some reason," she said in a husky voice that sent ripples up and down his spine.

"Naw, baby, it's not enough time right now. I want you to get on that phone and take care of my business for me," he stated again, still with his back to her.

Even though she hadn't put her hands on him, he could feel her presence. It was like an unwanted alien sending out brain waves that he couldn't cut off. The motivating forces were working, and it showed a weakness on his part. To let his woman have that much power over him was something he resented, while at the same time loving her even more for being able to cause him such a specific emotional disturbance. But it was a disturbance that he didn't want at the time because he had other things on his mind.

She took one more glance at her man and went over to the phone. She sat down on the bed with the telephone in her lap, looking at Kenyatta's stiff back. She couldn't understand why at times she felt as if he was fighting against her, not wanting to allow himself the pleasure of really loving her. Possibly, she thought, he was afraid that he might lose some of his power over her if he were to submit to her demanding love.

Betty dialed the number of the Twenty Grand Motel, but that came up a blank. She tried another motel, but this time she stopped and thought about the man she was trying to reach. The Creeper would probably be hiding in an out-of-the-way place, one that didn't have much traffic. Because of the crime he had committed, she figured he would want seclusion. His very soul should cry out for it, she reflected, as she remembered the news flash she had heard telling about the killing of the small children.

She had known at once that the Creeper was behind it. From conversations she had overheard between her man and that monster, she had put the crime at his doorstep. Nobody else in the organization could or would do something that vicious. Even Kenyatta had been shocked when he heard about it. It had been uncalled for. The death of the children was something that none of them wanted.

As she hesitated with the telephone cradled in her lap, it came to her in a flash. The dilapidated Kingsmen Motel, located over on Grand River Avenue near Davison Street, would be a good place for a man to hide. It was also one of the motels on their list of hideouts.

It took a minute to get Information to give her the number of the motel, and then she put through her call. "Hello," she said in that musical voice of hers. "Do you have a Mr. Marcus Gregory staying there? I don't know his room number, but I'm sure he checked in there sometime this week."

She waited a minute, then the desk man answered that he did have such a guest and put through the call. Suddenly a man's heavy voice was on the other end. "Just a minute," she replied, and held the phone out to Kenyatta, making sure she didn't use any name the switchboard operator could remember. It was bad enough making the call from the country. It could easily be traced if there was ever any need. But the Creeper kept his trail covered up so well she seriously doubted if there would ever be any need.

"What is it?" Kenyatta yelled into the receiver, then waited to make sure he had the person he wanted to talk to. "Listen, bro, I got something important for you, so when you pull up from that joint, stop at a pay phone and give me a ring, okay? Make it as soon as possible, 'cause it's important, my man," Kenyatta stated, then hung up the receiver, not bothering to wait to see if he was understood.

The person who didn't understand was the switchboard operator, who had kept his switchboard key open so that he could hear what was said. He was curious about the strange looking man who stayed in room 12. The man had moved like an animal. At first the operator had been frightened that the man might stick him up; then his curiosity had just got the best of him. The man in number 12 looked like a criminal to him, yet he hadn't done anything wrong. In fact, he paid his rent ahead of time and didn't bother him making silly phone calls all day long like some people.

But the police had asked him to listen in on conversations by people who seemed suspicious. The last time they had raided a room at the motel, they had asked him to listen in on any calls by some of the occupants who rented the high-priced rooms. No black person living honestly could afford those rates anyway. At least not the daily rates. At one time the motel had been used by affluent dope pushers, until the police came through and cleaned it out. Now the police used the switchboard operator to listen in, mainly on the ones who drove the long, expensive Cadillacs. It made him mad to see them pull up in the driveway. He knew that he would never be able to buy one of the luxurious cars and resented the long-haired black men who bought them as if they were small compact cars. Half of the niggers didn't work. He could tell that after they had stayed for a week or two, flashing their huge bankrolls every time they paid their rent.

There were two Cadillacs sitting in the driveway now, and one of the owners had two white girls with him, so the white operator knew that this was probably one of the many black pimps who came in and out. Now all he was waiting for was a chance to catch them with some white tricks in their room and he would call the vice squad immediately and bust their asses.

As the man who was going under the name of Marcus Gregory walked out of his room, the operator was trying to decide if it was important enough to call his buddy down on the vice squad. The only thing he had to go on was the fact that the caller had asked him to go out and find a pay phone.

He took a glance out the window just as the Creeper went by. One look at the ugly face on the man made up his mind for him. Any nigger who looked like that had to be up to something wrong. Why else would a woman first ask for him, then let a man take the phone, who then only ordered the ugly bastard to go out and find a pay phone? Yes, he reasoned, as he sat before his switchboard, something out of the ordinary was going on—he would be willing to bet his ass on it. The switchboard operator dialed police headquarters. He knew the number by heart.

Kenyatta sat on the bed rubbing the leg of the beautiful woman who was next to him. Betty stretched out on the bed with her arms thrown back over her head. Maybe, just maybe, she wished silently. For some reason, she couldn't get enough of this man. Kenyatta was her very life.

The telephone in their room rang shrilly. "Yeah," Kenyatta roared into the receiver. "Hang that motherfuckin' receiver up downstairs; I got the phone upstairs here!"

"Hey, baby boy, you at a pay phone now?" He waited for the reply, then continued. "Listen, brother, I got an important job for you, man. It's very important, and it's got to be taken care of immediately. Are you strapped down for business?"

The Creeper patted the gun under his armpit as if the man he was talking to could see his action. "I'm ready and willin', bro," he answered sharply.

"Good, then," Kenyatta replied quickly. "I want you to put a hit on this white sonofabitch Angelo. Angelo Benita will be the name he's under. The cat is staying at the Holiday Inn on Woodward in Highland Park. You know where the place is?" Again, Kenyatta waited for the Creeper's answer before continuing. "Now, dig this, bro," he said, making sure he never used the man's nickname because he sensed that the Creeper didn't like the name. "Okay, now dig this, boy. The fat honky is staying in room. . . ." He hesitated and dug out a small piece of paper from his pocket. "In room 204—that's right, 204. Now, he should be loaded with bread, but if you ain't got the time after makin' the hit, fuck the bread. Don't even worry about it, 'cause you ain't going there after the money. I want this fat-ass bastard dead before the fuckin' night is over. And listen, bro, I got this hunch that the motherfucker is about to split."

The Creeper asked a question and Kenyatta listened patiently before replying. "Yeah, you know him, bro; it's the same motherfucker we pick the guns up from. Yeah, well, the bastard has decided not to supply us with guns anymore, because of them hits you made on them bigshot honkies uptown. Yeah, it kind of got to Angelo so he's decided to freeze us out. That's right, bro, the honky don't want any more of our business, so I want his ass loaded up. Yeah, he's the one who sold us the motherfuckin' list; now he's gettin' an attitude because we're takin' care of business."

Kenyatta listened to the Creeper's heavy voice coming back over the wires, then cut him off. "You got enough bread to hold you, haven't you?" he inquired, then added after the man answered, "Good, that's enough cash for you if something should happen. You know, enough so that you can get around until I can get some more bread to you, but there's also the chance that you might catch Angelo on full, but you had better hurry.

Like I said, the peckerwood is gettin' ready to run. Yeah, I can smell it, plus the fact that I think he's going to try and sell us out to them dagos.

"Yeah, they'd love to know who's been knockin' their buddies off, but we ain't goin' give the snitch time to sell us down the drain—not if we can reach him in time. Yeah, so baby, you had better get on the case. Each minute we stand here rappin' about it gives the motherfucker that much more time to slide out of the trap we're about to spring on his white ass."

The telephone went dead in his ear and Kenyatta knew his instrument of death was on its way. If Angelo hadn't already run, he would not live to run tomorrow, because Creeper didn't miss. The man loved his work too much. The thought flashed through Kenyatta's mind about the children that the Creeper had knocked off, and he shrugged. It was something he hadn't foreseen. If he had, he would have given the man direct orders to leave the kids alone. They weren't old enough to hurt them, they couldn't identify him because of their age. So the man had killed them out of pleasure, and only pleasure. No one knew that better than Kenyatta.

After setting the telephone back on the bed, he turned to the woman lying next to him. He took her in his arms and kissed her gently, until his desire became stronger and his embrace tighter. He clutched her to him, feeling her passion matching his. He could think only of what he held in his arms. He pushed the red gown off her shoulders revealing her young, hard nipples. He planted a kiss on each one, nibbling slowly and tenderly.

Suddenly the door flew open. Ali stood there grinning down at the half-naked couple. "I heard you were up here in a business conference, and I thought that I'd come up and join the conference informally."

"Well," Kenyatta growled, his anger rising, "you see we're not in conference now, so how about closing the motherfuckin' door? This ain't no fuckin' peepshow for freaks," he added.

" 'Scuse me, boss, iff'n I's done wrong," Ali drawled with a put-on accent.

As Kenyatta rolled over in the bed and sat up, he could see the lust in Ali's eyes. The man still stood in the doorway, allowing his eyes to roam over Betty. He couldn't take his eyes off the woman.

"I ain't goin' ask you again to close that mother-fuckin' door," Kenyatta stated, the rage in his voice quite apparent.

"Okay, brother, just keep your shirt on," Ali said as he backed out of the door, his eyes still going over the woman's exposed breasts.

Even after the door was closed and the man was gone, the mood between the two people was broken. Kenyatta sat on the edge of the bed, brooding, trying to decide if he should follow Ali downstairs and bring things to a head. There was something building up between the two men. There was

something eating at the man, and it wouldn't let
go.

"Honey," Betty began, "please don't let it upset
you like that. You know what his problem is,
daddy. He just can't accept the idea that you're the
big fish in the pond and he's only a small one."

For a second he was tempted to go on downstairs, but the feel of her hands on his bare back,
her fingers moving slowly but surely, changed his
mind. He slumped back down on the king-sized
bed and tried to relax, yet the man's leering face
kept coming between him and what he was enjoying. Betty worked slowly. He could feel the slight
tug on his pants, then they were off. His shorts
came next, and then he stretched out and let himself enjoy the sensations his woman was sending
his way.

He closed his eyes as he felt something hot and
moist gripping his penis, and then he could feel
her tongue moving up and down the sides. The
sensation was almost unbearable at first. But then
he stretched back and really began to enjoy the
love his woman was making to him.

12

AS EVENING BEGAN TO FALL outside the motel,
Angelo moved swiftly around his room. It had
taken a while for him to make up his mind, but
now that it was made up, he knew he wanted to
get out of the city for a while. He couldn't understand what force was pushing him, but he was
used to playing his hunches. Now, a desperate
need to get away was upon him.

The desire to flee the city had come quite suddenly. Them crazy niggers was one thought that
came flashing back in his mind. He didn't have
any fear of what they might do to him, because he
couldn't see any reason for them to want to hurt
him. He had left that bastard Kenyatta up in the
air over the guns, not telling him straight out that
it was over with, just leading him on. He tried to
make him believe it would be a short period be-

fore they started doing business again. But he knew in his mind that they'd never do business again, not as long as he lived. Them niggers didn't have the sense God gave them, killing every fuckin' body in the city. All they were doing was causing a blood bath, killing like mad dogs.

For the thousandth time, he regretted that he had sold that list to Kenyatta. He hadn't had the slightest notion that the nigger would really follow up his big ideas. He couldn't imagine them spades really reaching the men he had put down on the list. Especially those three men whose names he had used just because they had been in the newspapers lately and everybody took them to be top Mafia men. He had known that none of the three had anything to do with dope. Now one of them was dead, and all because he had been pressed for money. If he had known, he could have put a couple of his debtors on the list. That way, he could have really got something out of it.

As he grabbed the last suits out of the closet, he glanced uneasily toward the doorway. What the hell was wrong with him tonight, he wondered. It wasn't like him to be nervous and jittery for no reason at all. He took another quick glance at his watch. He still had two hours to go before his plane left for Florida, so there was no rush. He had his rented car, and now all he had to do was put his few bags in the trunk and get on his way. It didn't take but twenty minutes to get to the airport, so he would still have over an hour and a half to kill. He couldn't see sitting out there all that time waiting for his plane to take off. Yet he still wanted to rush off.

Impatiently he snapped on the television, then tried to force himself to sit still and watch the six o'clock news. The killing of Kingfisher's men was the top story of the hour, and Angelo watched in shocked horror. He knew who had done it at once. The mention of the submachine guns put him right on their case. After that, the newsman gave a quick rundown on what had happened to the family of Mr. Kingfisher's bodyguard. Kingfisher was described as a "real-estate broker" who was being terrorized by someone in the city demanding money or his life.

Angelo cursed as he got up and began pacing. The mention of the atrocious way the bodyguard's children had been killed sent shivers up his spine. Which one of them bastards would have been behind that, he wondered. Since he knew so many of them, he tried to figure out which one of the niggers he knew could have done it. Then one face came into his mind. He pictured the one they called "the Creeper" as he had seen the man the last time, when he had come to pick up some guns. A shiver ran down his back and he decided he would feel much better being out at the airport with people around him. He could go into the bar and get himself juiced up.

Angelo's mind wouldn't allow him to relax, so he started moving the few bags next to the door.

As he went back into the bathroom to get his shaving kit, he wondered if he could sell the information to one of the big boys without getting himself involved. If he came out and told them he had supplied the guns to the niggers, they would put two and two together and come up with his name bigger than shit.

By now, they must have realized that someone had a list with quite a few of the big shots' names on it. The big boys were walking around in a daze hoping like hell their names weren't on that list. So it wouldn't do, no matter how he toyed with the idea, to let them know that he knew the niggers responsible for the mass murders. He couldn't afford to sell his knowledge. Those people played pretty damn rough. They wouldn't accept his denial that he didn't know anything about the list. No, they wouldn't believe him, not if he gave them even a hint of what he knew.

Next, he considered the possibility of calling the police and leaving a tip. The idea intrigued him. Something had to be done. A mad dog had been turned loose, and no matter how he thought about it, Angelo felt as if he were responsible.

Angelo came out of the bathroom with his mind made up. He picked up the telephone and made his call. He asked for the homicide division and spoke hurriedly when the detective answered.

"If you want to know who's behind these killings, check out some punks that have an organization on Clay Street. Their leader is called

Kenyatta. I know from personal experience that Kenyatta's people are responsible for the killings that happened today. I saw the submachine guns when they put them in their car."

He quickly hung up, then wiped the sweat off his brow. He smiled, feeling as if he had done at least one good turn today. What was it Kenyatta called him—a snitch? *Well, Kenyatta, old boy, I guess you can really call me a snitch now. I just hope they bust your black ass as soon as possible.*

Down at headquarters, Detective Nelson called his partner, Steward, over and whispered the information in his ear. Both men got up and slipped out of the office. This was the break they needed. Nelson held a small piece of paper in his hand. "The caller even gave me this address. It won't take us long to check it out. He says they keep their guns hid there, too."

Steward glanced over at him. "You think we might meet with more than we can handle? Maybe we should take some kind of help along."

"Fuck that shit!" Nelson exploded. "I don't plan on allowing none of those bastards to steal this shit from under our noses. Hell no, we can check it out ourselves, and if we need any help, call in a black-and-white squad car as a backup. In fact, when we get there, we can call in a couple of squad cars to help us out."

The two detectives grinned at each other and rushed down in the elevator. This was a chance to put a feather in each of their caps—ones they could be proud of. The captain would have to look at them with a little more respect after this, instead of putting all his faith in that black and white team he seemed to favor.

As the two detectives left the elevator downstairs in the basement garage, they met Detectives Malloy and Andrews of Vice. Nelson and Steward stopped and waited for the other young detectives to reach them. Steward leaned back on his heels and opened his suitcoat, revealing the double-harness shoulder holster he wore. The two big forty-fives made his suitcoat lopsided.

"When the hell did you start working with Wild Bill Hickok, Nelson?" Detective Malloy asked as they came up.

Nelson just smiled, then said, "Jack, you know how Steward is. He thinks two of everything is better than one, but I'd be damned if I'd want to lug all that heavy artillery around. This fuckin' thirty-eight I have to carry gets in the way too damn much as it is."

Steward only chuckled. He didn't give a damn what they thought about him wearing two pistols. He liked the idea of himself in his checkered red-and-white sports coat with the two guns underneath.

Malloy ignored the young detective after that and spoke to Nelson. "I think I might have something for you. It's only a small lead, but it might just click. We got a call from this informant of ours at a motel over on Grand River. Now, I don't know if it will help you or not, or even if it's your man, because we got this call and just ran by there and checked the guy's room out. There wasn't nothing there, but one thing kept ringing in my mind. I heard about this description you got from the paperboy on that family killing out in Conant Gardens." Malloy hesitated, then added, "It might be nothing, but it rang this bell with me, you know, with the kid calling the guy he saw leaving the house a creeper. Well, we got the very same description from the motel owner, you know. The only way he can describe this guy is by calling him a creeper. So, like I said, it might not be anything, but it is funny that both people resorted to the same description. I mean, it's different—you don't run into it every day, so he must be a hard-lookin' fucker whoever he is." Jack gestured with his hands. "But like I said, it might be nothing; then again, it might give you guys a lead. From what I hear, you could sure as hell stand a lead right about now."

Malloy's partner, Andrews, spoke up. "I wanted to find Ryan and let him know about this. He digs like a bulldog, so something like this would be right up his line."

"Goddamn it, Andrews, you don't have to tell Ryan shit," Steward said, letting his coat fall back in place as he stopped posing. "Me and Nelson can check it out as good as Ryan and that spade he works with."

Andrews glanced sharply at Steward. "I don't know how you meant that, Steward, but I'll tell you one thing. Benson, that so-called spade, is one of the best detectives you'll ever meet, and you can lay odds to that."

At that moment, Steward snorted through his nose as if he'd just gotten a smell of something bad. "Each man to his own opinion, Tom, but I have my doubts about Mr. Benson. He don't raise no hell in my view. I don't see him bustin' this case we're all workin' like hell to open. Naw, he's just living off of past cases. You guys will see one day, if it weren't for the old boy Ryan, that spade would probably still be in uniform someplace."

"Well, whatever you do," Malloy stated harshly, "don't let Ryan hear you cuttin' his partner up like that, because you'd have one mad-ass officer on your tail!"

"I wouldn't blame him, either," Andrews added. "Benson has saved Ryan's life on more than one occasion, Steward. And Ryan don't forget things like that. Especially when a guy steps in front of you and takes a fuckin' slug from a thirty-eight in his own chest so that you don't get hit."

"That's new shit to me," Nelson said, trying to pull his partner out of the hot water he was getting into.

"Yeah, it probably is, but the old-timers around here know about it," Malloy stated coldly. "It was before you guys' time. Both of you were still in school when it happened. And Ryan is one guy who will never forget it. He looks on his colored partner as a friend, so keep that in mind whenever you're talking about Benson around him. He won't stand for no shit said about his partner, and when I say he won't stand for it, I mean just that. It don't take much to set him off, either." Malloy turned to his partner. "Well, Tom, we gave these guys enough to make them heroes if they follow it up right, so let's get on upstairs and finish our checker game."

Steward laughed. "That's the sweet thing about vice detail. All you guys have to do is bust some sweet-ass broads and relax the rest of the time."

"Yeah, you hit it right on the head," Malloy answered sharply. "That's all we have to do. But if I were you," and again he turned to Nelson. "I'd approach this guy with a lot of care. We just left the motel and it looks as if he will be coming back there, but we didn't have any jurisdiction, so we left. So we decided to pass the information on to you guys, who get paid for working on this kind of crap."

"Okay, we really appreciate it," Nelson said as the two men started to walk away. "And we'll check it out. You never can tell; it might just be the key we've been looking for."

"I'll just bet it is," the two vice men heard Steward say dryly as the men went off in pairs.

"You know," Malloy said loud enough for Steward and Nelson to hear, "that fuckin' Steward is a smart-ass bastard. I'd sure in the hell hate to be in

Nelson's position and have to work with that smart-ass every day. Jesus Christ, I couldn't wish that on my worst friend, if you know what I mean."

Nelson had to reach out and grab Steward's arm to hold him back. "Don't worry about cracks like that, man. We got more important things on our minds than what some fuckin' frustrated vice squad dick says. Let's get over there and see if we can shed some kind of light on this case, Stew. With both these leads we got, maybe, just maybe one of them might pay off."

"Okay," Steward answered. "I'll say amen to that. But when we get back, I'm going to ask that smart ass just what he meant by that crack, and you can bet on that."

13

THE CREEPER PEERED OUT of his motel room window. The room he had rented at the Holiday Inn was right across from the one that was still occupied by Angelo. From what he could see through the partially open drapes of Angelo's window, he could tell that the man was getting ready to make his run.

Kenyatta hadn't been wrong about that, he reflected as he watched. The bastard is on his way out as quick as he can go, but ain't he got a surprise coming? He ain't going where he's expectin' to go, the Creeper coldly thought as he watched and waited, trying to make up his mind how to do it. He didn't like to make his hits out in the open, but at the rate Angelo was moving, it looked as if he would have to knock the sucker off out in the parking lot.

Suddenly out of the corner of his eyes, he noticed some movement. It was the maid going into an apartment four doors down from the one that Angelo occupied. It came to him at once. The idea was beautiful. He found himself moving before he had even finished thinking it through. It would work, he was sure of it.

He ran down the stairway and up the steps into the other wing. He slowed down as he approached the open door where the maid was busy making up the bed. The heavyset black woman had her back turned to him as he slipped into the room. She must have sensed his presence because she was turning around when he chopped down on the back of her neck with a judo punch. It was a neck-breaking blow, one that the Creeper knew how to deliver with ease. He was always surprised whenever he used it and killed with just the one blow. It made his pride swell to know that he could take a life with just one simple action.

The dead black woman meant nothing to him. He had no emotional feelings about killing her other than a feeling of pride—pride that he could destroy with just one well-placed blow to the back of the neck. He owed this prowess to what Kenyatta had taught him.

He reached down and took the key ring from the woman's body, examining his work and nodding silently. *The bitch never knew what hit her.* He chuckled, remembering the long hours he had spent listening to Kenyatta, then doing the things that his leader had instructed him to do. *Yeah,* thought the Creeper, *that's one black man who really knows his shit.*

The Creeper moved quietly to the door, took a quick glance outside to make sure the way was clear, and then slipped out, closing the door firmly behind him. It would be a while before anybody found the woman's body; then it would be too late. He would be long gone. The job that was waiting for him was the one he was concerned with, and he only hoped it would go as smoothly as the murder of the maid. If he could kill the fat man with one blow, there would be no noise to give him away. It would be the perfect murder.

He checked the numbers on the key ring until he found the one he wanted. He hesitated outside the door of Angelo's room, listening. He wanted to make sure the man was by himself. He'd hate to bust in and find some cunt lying up on the bed. Quietly he inserted the key in the lock, and removed the pistol from his shoulder holster. He put his shoulder against the door and pushed. He was in the room before the fat man had any idea he was going to have company.

Angelo glanced up sharply as he heard his door open. His jaw dropped in surprise as he saw the tall, baldheaded man step into the room. The big gun in the black man's hand told him it wasn't a friendly visit. Just the sight of the Creeper caused Angelo to feel as if he was about to have a bowel movement.

"What the fuck's going on here?" he managed to say, trying to get up from the edge of the bed. His legs didn't have any strength in them, so he just sat back down.

"Hello, white boy. You didn't think we were goin' let you leave town with all our money, did you?" the Creeper inquired, as his small reddish eyes searched the room, making sure no one else was there. "Naw, man, we couldn't allow no shit like that. So Kenyatta sent me around to collect it. He says you sold him some bullshit information, some shit he can't use. It seems as if every fuckin' body on the list you gave him is dying for some reason or other." The man let out a cold laugh.

The Creeper leaned over towards Angelo, as if he was going to confide in him. "Yeah, Angelo, ol' boy, as much trouble as we've gone through, it would seem that you would know better than to put shit on my main man like that, so here I am. The collector. I've come to pick up the money you came and collected for a list that wasn't worth a shit."

For a brief second, Angelo felt relief. If it wasn't nothing but a heist, it wouldn't be bad. He could always get some more money, even though he hated the idea of parting with what he had. It was what he had planned to use on his trip, but from the looks of the black man in front of him, this was no time to argue over a few thousand.

"So that's how you guys operate. After all the fuckin' guns I've sold you, you turn around and rip me off. You know, you can tell Kenyatta for me that this ends our gun connection. He'll never get another fuckin' thing out of me."

Angelo was just talking now, trying to make himself believe that nothing more than a heist was going on. His mind wouldn't accept any other idea. It couldn't all come to an end like this. Not in a fuckin' motel room, at the hands of a goddamn nigger. No, he couldn't bring himself to face it.

Angelo got up and walked over to his suitcase.

"Now, don't make no sudden moves while you're playin' around there," Creeper warned him sharply as he came around the bed behind him.

Shivers went up and down Angelo's spine at the nearness of the man. "I'm just gettin' the fuckin' money for you. Ain't that what you said you came for?" Angelo snapped, trying to muster up the courage he didn't have. He could hardly stand because his knees were shaking so badly. He pulled out a package of money, wrapped with the amount written across the paper. As he did this, he tried to cover up another package of money that was of the same amount.

"Here, take it; it's five grand there. Just what Kenyatta paid for the list. Tell him for me that I've got a hell of a shipment of guns coming, and I know he'll want them. But before he can get them, he'll have to kick back this bread that you're rippin' me off for. I mean every fuckin' word of it, too," Angelo said, fooling no one but himself, unable to face the fact that he would never leave that room alive.

The small pistol that he had hidden at the bottom of his suitcase stayed right there. He just didn't have the nerve to try for it. At least not while he believed he might be able to talk his way out of the situation.

The Creeper studied him icily. "You know, the way you pulled that package out, I have a feeling it's not the only money you have there. I mean, I wouldn't be able to sleep nights if I thought I left with only half the money while you still had more."

Angelo turned on him angrily, "Just what the hell is this? A rip-off? You said you came after the five grand that Kenyatta paid for the list!" Angelo found courage in his desperation. The prospect of losing all of his money affected the fat man deeply.

"What do you really think it is, white boy?" Creeper said, as he pulled the razor out of his pocket and advanced towards the frightened man.

It was out in the open now. This man had come to kill him. Angelo stalled for time. "Wait, here, I'll give you all the money, just don't cut me." Angelo wasn't truly a coward. He had come up in the old school with some of the meanest dagos the city had ever produced, but this one black man had made him lose his balls for a minute. Now, faced with certain death, his courage returned. It was the courage of a cornered rat.

"I got ten thousand dollars more here," Angelo said abruptly, hoping he could fool the man who had come to kill him.

"Ten grand more!" the Creeper shouted. That was more money than he had ever seen in his life. Even though he didn't care that much about money, he knew that, if he returned with fifteen thousand dollars, Kenyatta would be pleased as hell. As these thoughts flew through his mind, Creeper made one of the first big mistakes he had made since becoming a professional hit man; he took his eyes off the fat man. Angelo took out the other package of money and tossed it on the bed, then went back to looking in the suitcase as if he was searching for another one.

The bundle of money hit the bed and fell to the floor. The Creeper's eyes followed the package, noticing that it was wrapped like the one he had already stuck in his pocket. There was writing on the wrapping, and as he reached down and picked it up, he could see that the amount was five thousand dollars.

While mentally counting the money, the Creeper believed that the frightened fat man was searching for a third package. With that one, he would have the fifteen grand the man said he had, and then he could get on with cutting the honky's throat.

He was just straightening up from picking up the package when the fat man made his move. Angelo spun around, swinging the suitcase, and as the suitcase struck the Creeper in the chest, the fat man raised the small Derringer he had palmed and fired. The suitcase seemed to have done more damage to the Creeper than the little gun. The two quick shots that struck him in the stomach didn't faze him at all. He raised the thirty-eight in his left hand, dropping the straight razor to the floor.

The sound of the police special going off in the small room was deafening. The first shot caught Angelo high in the chest, slamming him back against the wall. The second shot struck two inches away from the first one.

As Angelo struggled to raise the small pistol, he remembered that it was only a two-shot Derringer. The gun clicked on empty chambers.

As the Creeper turned away from the dying man, he could feel the pain starting to spread in his stomach. He clutched at his guts and staggered around the big bed. He noticed a towel lying on the top of the end table and snatched it up. He stuck it inside his shirt, trying to stop the flow of blood, cursing loudly. "The sonofabitching honky faked me out," he murmured as he started to make his way from the room.

His mind was racing. He knew he would have to get away, and quick. The sounds of his thirty-eight going off had been loud enough to awaken the dead. He staggered to the door and somehow managed to snatch it open. As he stumbled from the room, still clutching the thirty-eight tightly in his fist, he struggled to reach the iron railing and caught his balance. Out of the corner of his eye, he could make out two men rushing up the stairway. His brain warned him that it was the police. He realized at once that he couldn't outrun them. He raised the gun up as the first officer came up the steps.

For some reason he couldn't seem to draw his bead on the man, who stopped and yelled, "Drop it, police!" That was the only warning he got. The second man, who appeared to be a black man, raised his weapon and fired. The shot picked him up and threw him backwards. He could feel himself falling, and then the concrete struck him in the back.

"Goddamn it, Ben, I wanted to take him alive." The Creeper heard the words coming as if they were from a great distance. Even then he attempted to raise the gun in his hand. But someone kicked the weapon away.

"Yeah, I know; you wanted him alive bad enough to get shot up for it," Benson said sharply, bending over the Creeper's body. "Looks as if somebody else shot him before I hit him," Benson said after making a quick examination.

Ryan took a quick look inside the motel room. "There's another one inside. I better check and find out if he's cashed in his chips yet." He went inside and leaned down over Angelo.

When Angelo tried to speak, blood came gushing out of his mouth. "I'm on my last ride," he

managed to say.

"Who's responsible for this?," Ryan asked Angelo sharply, almost pulling the wounded man up to his feet. He bent down and listened as the man tried to speak. "It's that fuckin' Kenyatta. He's gone mad. I shouldn't have ever sold him that list." Again blood came out of the man's mouth. "All my fault. . . . I sold him the fuckin' list."

"Where can we find Kenyatta? Where, Angelo, where the hell does he hide out?"

At first Ryan thought the question would go unanswered, but somehow the man managed to raise up on his elbow and speak. "Farm, he's got a farm," but as he tried to give the information, he coughed up the last life in his body. Dark blood ran down his chin.

Ryan didn't need a doctor to tell him that the man was dead.

14

DETECTIVES NELSON and Steward decided to give up the stakeout on the motel. After all, they were sitting around waiting for a man they weren't sure they wanted. When the call came over their two-way radio about the shoot-out at the Holiday Inn, they decided to drive over and check it out. Upon their arrival, the first thing they noticed was the car belonging to Detectives Benson and Ryan.

"We should have known these bastards would be up on the fuckin' shoot-out," Nelson growled as he tried to find a place to park.

Had the two detectives not been so busy cursing out their rivals, they would have noticed the two well-dressed black couples making their way out of the crowd of curious onlookers around the courtyard. What was so peculiar about the two couples was that both men, and one of the women, had their hair completely shaved off. Their heads shone with some kind of lotion beneath the bright neon lights.

The two couples hurried away from the crowd toward a parked car near the parking lot of the Holiday Inn. Neither detective noticed because they were too busy with their petty jealousy.

"These fuckin' guys get all the breaks," Detective Steward said before getting out of the car.

As Detectives Nelson and Steward bellyached to each other, the four members of Kenyatta's organization made their way to their car. It was of the utmost importance that they reach Kenyatta at once to let him know what had just happened at the motel. Their orders had been to check into the Holiday Inn to make sure Kenyatta's orders had been carried out. Only one of them had known what the leader's orders had been. But with the killing of their best hit man, whom all of them recognized on sight, they knew something had gone wrong.

They had stayed long enough to find out just what had happened inside the room. They knew the white man and the black maid had been killed. This they had witnessed themselves. Eddie-Bee had been at the window and had seen the Creeper when he slipped in the open doorway behind the maid's back. And afterwards, while the Creeper was busy elsewhere, Jug had run over to check it out, bringing back the news that the elderly black woman was, indeed, dead.

Jug settled his lean, angular body into the driver's seat of the rented black Chevy and started the motor. Eddie-Bee got into the backseat with his woman. Each man had brought his girlfriend along to make it look legitimate when they checked into the double suite at the motel.

For Eddie-Bee, who had been in on the holdup of the stamp place, this was a cakewalk. He only wished all his assignments were this easy.

"As soon as you see a pay phone, pull over," Eddie-Bee ordered loudly from the rear of the car.

"Hey, man," Jug yelled back, resenting the idea of the man telling him what was obvious. "When I need some advice I'll ask for it, okay? But telling me what any fool would realize is something I don't appreciate."

From the tone of Jug's voice, Eddie-Bee realized he had overstepped the bounds in trying to be helpful. "Okay, baby, don't get no attitude," Eddie-Bee said quickly. "I was just trying to be helpful, that's all."

"There's a pay phone over on your right," Jug's girlfriend Almeta stated. She was rather tall, and completely bald, just like her man. If it wasn't for her huge chest, people would take her for a man at first glance.

After a quick look, Jug swung to the curb next to the phone booth. Almeta had trouble beating

Eddie-Bee out of the car because he tried to push the seat up so that he could get out first.

"Slow down, man," Jug cautioned. "It don't make no difference which one of us makes the report. We're all together on this job, so just be cool. You ain't goin' gain nothing or lose nothing by being the one to report it to Kenyatta."

Eddie-Bee sat back in his seat. He wished he had been the one to break the news to Kenyatta, but it had been impossible to get out of the car before Almeta.

After one more cold glance at the man in the rear, Jug shook his head in disgust. "I don't know how you put up with such a nigger, Penny," he stated, looking at Eddie-Bee's woman in his rearview mirror.

Penny just shook her head. "You know it's a man shortage in the streets, Jug, so sometimes a girl has to take what comes along." She laughed to take the sting out of her words.

It didn't take but two or three minutes before Almeta rejoined them in the car. "I got in touch with Kenyatta," she stated breathlessly, as if she had just run a mile, "but Ali answered the phone, and do you know that nigger didn't want to put Kenyatta on the line until I told him what it was about. I mean, he just wouldn't call Kenyatta."

She sounded dumbfounded about the situation but continued. "I know he'd like to take Kenyatta's place, but if he was in charge, I'd quit. Just like that, I'd give up the organization, because he's too much for me. He thinks he's too pretty, first of all. Then he believes he's the only person with any sense. Ain't nobody else got no brains but him, if you listen to him. That's the impression he gives me anyway."

"Shit!" Penny sighed loudly. "I think Ali's one fine black nigger, if you ask me."

"It's a good thing didn't nobody ask you then," Eddie-Bee stated coldly, his anger showing in his voice.

"Aw, honey," Penny said, rubbing his jaw, "ain't no reason you gettin' jealous, 'cause as long as you're around, there ain't no room in my heart for no other man."

"I'll bet," Jug said under his breath so that the rest of them didn't hear. "What did Kenyatta say after you gave him the news?" he inquired loudly.

"Oh . . . ," Almeta moaned, surprised by the simple question. "He wants us to get out to the farm at once. It took him by surprise that the Creeper got himself killed, but not me. I'm glad the dirty, murdering sonofabitch is dead." She spoke with more venom than she realized. "I couldn't stand the sight of him as it was. Then after those murders he did, shit. Well, all I got to say is I hope don't nobody else join our organization like him. I ain't never seen no man like him before, and I hope I don't live long enough to meet another one."

"I'll say amen to that," Penny replied quickly.

"He was a murdering bastard at that. There was no reason for him to kill that maid. Did you tell Kenyatta about him killin' the maid?"

"No, there was no time for that," Almeta replied softly. "As soon as I told him about Creeper gettin' cut down as he came out of the motel room, he wanted to know if the Creeper took care of his homework, to which I replied yes. I was sure of that. They carried the fat man out on a long stretcher with his face covered up. I didn't see his face, like I told him, but from the shape on that stretcher, it had to be fat boy. Couldn't nobody else have a belly stickin' up in the air like that."

Suddenly Jug made a sharp turn off Woodward. "I want to hit the freeway as soon as possible. I think we had better get out to the farm fast. Things might start jumping around town, and everybody will have to go in hiding." Jug meticulously picked his way through the evening traffic.

Almeta rolled her window up. "Damn if it ain't gettin' chilly out," she stated. "I don't know if it's all that safe at the farm. What do you think about it, Jug?"

"Well, I'm on my way out there, whether or not it's safe. We've made plans in case this kind of thing happened. If it comes down to it, we just go into what Kenyatta calls 'Operation Break-Out.' We all know about it, so now will be the time to put it into action—if it comes to that."

His words brought silence to the people in

the car. Each one was filled with his or her own thoughts. No one really wanted to go through with the so-called "Operation Break-Out," but it had been planned, and everybody knew what their roles in it would be.

While the car with its four occupants fled towards the outskirts of town, two detectives back at the motel were trying to wrap up the case.

Benson walked into the room, feeling the two heavy packages of money he had removed from the dead man's body in his pockets. He was still undecided on whether or not to give one of them to his partner. "Did you get anything out of your man before he died?" he inquired of Ryan.

Ryan looked up tiredly. "I don't know, Ben. He mentioned something about a farm, but that was about it. What about your man out there? Did he have anything to say before he passed on to the hell waiting for him?"

Benson managed to grin. "Yeah, he managed to gain enough strength to spit in my face before he kicked off," Benson answered truthfully. "That bastard was mean through and through. I don't think there was a kind streak in him anywhere."

"I'm inclined to believe you there. But it looks like he made a mistake about our boy Angelo here. It turns out Angelo was a little bit rougher than he had thought." Ryan held up the little pee-shooter Angelo had used to punch two holes in the Creeper's belly. "He hit his man, didn't he?"

"Yeah," Benson answered, "it's like I told you. It wasn't just my shot that put him away. When we saw him reeling, it was from them two shots he had in his gut."

As the other policemen began pouring into the small motel room, Ryan asked his partner if he had found anything of value on the dead man.

Benson shrugged. "It depends on what you call value." He nodded his head towards the toilet. "Let's step in the men's room for a minute. I got something I'd like to show you."

Ryan followed his partner into the bathroom. Neither man spoke until Benson closed the door and leaned against it.

"Well, what is it? Did the guy give us a lead?" Ryan asked impatiently.

"Naw, it ain't no fuckin' lead," Benson replied, then removed one bundle of money from his pocket and tossed it towards his partner. "He did have that on him, so I wondered if you and I could use it, or should we turn it in for evidence that will never be used?"

For the next five minutes Benson watched his friend and partner change expressions. "Not me, Ben. What do you want to do about it?"

Without realizing it, Benson fingered the other bank notes in his pocket. He knew what he was going to do. This time he would come out with something if the captain should ever make good on one of his many threats to remove him from his position. Whatever Ryan decided to do with the bundle of money he had tossed to him was all right with him, but the one in his pocket was going to stay there.

"No, Ryan, it's not my decision. If I was going to keep it for myself, you would never have known. But I wanted you up on it. It's a nice piece of money, and nobody will miss it. If you want to, we can split it up between us. If not, turn it in, but don't ask me to make the decision. That way, if you have guilty thoughts later on, I don't want you blaming me. I'll go along with you either way. I could use the money, and so could you, but it's your baby. Make up your own mind."

"Goddamn it, Ben, why the hell do you do these kind of things to me? Ain't I got enough problems worrying about this fuckin' case without you tossin' temptation in front of me like this?"

"We ain't gettin' no younger, Ryan. If something bad should happen to either one of us, this would go a long way towards helpin' the few people in the world who mean anything to us."

It took a second, but finally a sheepish grin broke out over Ryan's face. "Well, I guess it ain't like being on the take. It must have been the money the bastard got for trying to make the hit on Angelo."

The two men stared at each other, and finally Benson broke the silence. "Then I take it, you'll go along with holding back this small sum for ourselves?"

Ryan shook his head undecidedly. "I just don't know yet, Ben. Let's sit on it for a while, okay?"

Their eyes met, and then Ryan glanced away, but not before Benson could read the greed there. Ryan wanted the money, but just didn't know how to go about keeping it. His conscience would bother him for a while, but Benson was sure he would get over it.

A sudden commotion in the outer room brought both detectives rushing out. To their astonishment they found Nelson and Steward there, trying to take charge.

"Hold on, boys," Ryan said harshly. "I've already given these men their orders, so don't interfere. This is our little problem, so you guys just take a backseat."

As the detectives dickered among themselves, Kenyatta was busy making calls from his farm. He was also making one final decision—one that involved the Kingfisher.

"Listen, Jerry, I've tried every way possible to get this hit made without using you. But I put you in the position you're in, just in case something like this came up. Well, it's up. There is no other way out of this. Either you make the hit on the Kingfisher or the bastard gets away."

There was silence on the other end of the line. For a minute Kenyatta wondered if the man had hung up. But then he spoke in a low voice. "Well, what do you want me to do?"

"Do?" Kenyatta roared. "Why, I want you to assassinate the bastard. Shoot the motherfucker down like the dog that he is. If you do this, Jerry, you'll save hundreds of black lives—hundreds!" Kenyatta did not add that the man would also be giving up his own life when he followed through with the order.

"How?" Jerry asked.

To Kenyatta the question was too simple. It showed that the man wasn't using his head. It might benefit Jerry to act like he was a robot sometimes, but Kenyatta knew that this job required a man to use his brain.

"How!" Kenyatta repeated loudly. "Man, you're not even trying to think, Jerry. I got you that job there in the apartment building because you were one of my best trained men, and most faithful. Remember your baby sister dying from the overdose?"

Kenyatta knew that should be enough to convince him, but he continued anyway. "Well, I can damn near prove the dope came from the Kingfisher, but all that shit ain't necessary. Either you're going to do it or not. If you are, this is all you have to do. When the Kingfisher and his men come back downstairs, you get as close as possible and cut loose with that thirty-eight I gave you. As good a shot as you are, it shouldn't take but one shitty-ass shot, but I want you to be sure to hit him twice. You got that, Jerry? When he comes out through the lobby, you're to make your hit!"

This time there was a long silence before the

man finally spoke. "I understand, Kenyatta. This is what I've been trained for, so I'll do it. I'm as dedicated as anybody else in the organization."

"Good. Just make sure you don't miss, Jerry. Make damn sure you don't miss. And don't forget, put two slugs in his dope-selling ass. You hear me? One for your sister and one for the rest of the kids who have died from the poison his men have been selling in our neighborhoods."

Kenyatta waited until the man answered affirmatively. "Okay, then. When you hang up, go get your piece. You ain't got no time to waste. We want this bastard dead before he receives the new shipment of dope coming in. We can't cut the shipment off, but if we hit the Kingfisher, he won't be able to distribute that fuckin' poison!"

After hanging up the telephone, Jerry moved as if he was under some kind of spell. First, he went down to the locker room and opened up his locker. From it he took out the still-new thirty-eight automatic. The gun shined from constant polishing. It had never been fired. He picked out six bullets from a full box, then put the rest back into his locker. He laid the gun and bullets out on the bench that he used when changing in and out of his work clothes.

After he finished putting on his fresh bellboy uniform, Jerry had trouble figuring out where to put the gun. If he stuck it in his belt, it would make a bulge. He might be able to conceal it under his arm, but he didn't have a shoulder holster to make it stay in place. He sat down on the bench for ten minutes trying to figure out what to do with the gun.

Suddenly he got an idea. He stood up, put the gun in his belt, next to the small part of his back, then pulled his coat down over it. It didn't seem to bulge too much, and if he kept his back turned, nobody would notice it anyway. At last Jerry was ready. At no time had he doubted that he would go through with his assignment. This was what he had been trained for, his purpose in being here. He made his way back up the steps with swiftness and certainty. He was now a dedicated man with a mission.

It happened sooner than he hoped for. Jerry hadn't been in the lobby more than forty minutes when the private elevator that handled only the Kingfisher's penthouse began to come down. Jerry watched the dial as it moved lower and lower.

Kingfisher stood in the elevator smiling. He had heard the news on the television and had watched the film clips of the bodies being removed from the Holiday Inn. He knew the identity of the man the Creeper had gunned down. Just a short time earlier he had put through a call and had told some big men his idea about somebody selling guns to the blacks in the ghetto, and the name "Angelo" had been one of those mentioned as the possible seller. As soon as this had been brought to the big men's attention, they had made the logical connections. Whoever supplied the guns was more than likely the same man who supplied the blacks with the list of people bringing dope into the city.

Now that the gun runner was dead, it wouldn't take long before the men who had bought the guns would be out searching for another connect, thus exposing themselves. When they did, they would be taken care of. To celebrate, the Kingfisher was taking everybody in his place out on the town.

Vickie, the Kingfisher's special woman, smiled broadly for the first time in what seemed like months, fussing over which expensive gown she should wear—the gold one or the navy blue one that looked good with the string of pearls Kingfisher had bought for her. She decided to wear the low-cut gold gown. It revealed more in the front and back.

She dressed with care. It had been so long, so goddamn long since they had been anywhere. She could hear Kingfisher singing in the bedroom as he dressed. What a time they would have tonight. It seemed as if they had been living under the shadow of fear for so long that they had been tempted to run off. Just pack a few of the expensive things Kingfisher had bought for her and leave town. The news on the television meant that was all over now and everybody seemed happy.

"Let's go," the Kingfisher called out happily. It

had been quite a while since anyone had seen him in such a good mood.

Vickie rushed out of the bedroom and joined the rest of the party at the elevator. They waited while one of the bodyguards used his key to open up the doors. Then the small party of five people walked in. Besides Vickie and Kingfisher, there were three bodyguards going along. It was quite a cutback from the time when the Kingfisher wouldn't go out with fewer than six bodyguards.

As soon as the elevator door opened at the ground floor, the bodyguards got out. They didn't notice anything out of the ordinary. The bellboy standing near the door was the same one they had seen many times before.

As Kingfisher stepped from the elevator with a big smile on his face, he noticed the youthful bellboy start towards them.

Jerry reached behind his back, and the next thing Kingfisher saw was the long barrel of a thirty-eight automatic pointed directly at him. His heart froze. The warning yell he gave to his bodyguards was too late. He attempted to duck behind his woman. Vickie let out a scream of fear as she felt Kingfisher trying to use her for a shield. But the young gunman wouldn't be denied. He pushed the gun in Kingfisher's face and pulled the trigger.

The roar of the thirty-eight was deafening, as were the answering shots that cut the young boy down in his tracks.

The Kingfisher's body had slid down the wall. The bellboy had been struck from two different sides. Kingfisher's bodyguards were not slow; they had just been taken completely by surprise. The two shots fired by the bellboy had struck the Kingfisher high in the neck. He had been dead before he reached the luxurious carpet. Kingfisher didn't live long enough to know that his bodyguards had done their job, at least avenging him, if not managing to protect him.

15

AS THE POLICE LEFT Kenyatta's club on the north side of Detroit and headed towards the farm in the country, some of the people on the farm were making hurried efforts to leave. As soon as the club had been raided, Kenyatta had been called and duly informed. The few members inside the club hadn't stood up too long before giving out the information on Kenyatta's whereabouts, but that was something Kenyatta had expected.

Kenyatta was well armed when he left the farm, taking four men with him. Each of the men took his woman along in one of the two cars—Jug and his girlfriend, Almeta; Eddie-Bee with his lady, and Red and Arlene, the woman who had gotten rid of the guns for them after the holdup.

Kenyatta and Betty, with over thirty thousand

dollars in a black briefcase between them, rode with Zeke and his black queen. Each couple was armed to the teeth, men and women alike, as they pulled out of the farmyard.

The rest of the people watched them go, not knowing when their leader would return. Ali stood at the front door scratching his chin. He had been left in charge, and that was all that mattered to him, but he could feel something wrong. He couldn't know that his rule would last only a few hours.

Ali didn't have the knowledge that Kenyatta possessed. He was uninformed about the raid on the city clubhouse, and he didn't know that an army of police were on their way to the farm at that very moment.

When Kenyatta and his group reached the airport, they parked the cars in a no-standing zone, abandoning them. None of them had any thoughts of returning that way. It was time to get out. It was a well thought-out plan of escape. Now was the time to put it to use.

Everybody followed Kenyatta into the airport. As he bypassed the ticket windows, he turned and joked with his followers. "Now that sure in the hell would be a waste of money, wouldn't it?" he said as he shifted the heavy black bag around in his left hand.

All of the women carried big, heavy shoulder-bags. Each couple carried a certain amount of cash on them, in case they ran into more trouble than they could handle and had to split up, but none of them had as much as Kenyatta carried.

They waited about ten minutes until people started boarding a nonstop flight to California, then Kenyatta led his small group toward the loading ramp. The airport was set up in such a way that they didn't check for weapons until a person was going onto the ramp that led into the plane. Here a few guards stood around looking bored, watching the metal detector to see if anyone was possibly carrying a weapon.

When Kenyatta's group reached them, there was no suspicion because the group was well-dressed and smiling. They came up to the ramp as if they had tickets, then all at once hell broke loose. Kenyatta pulled out an automatic. He waved it at the guards as his people came rushing up beside him. With a wave of his hand, he sent Red rushing up the ramp.

The sight of the black men trying to commandeer the plane sent the guards into action. As Red came rushing up, one tried to reach out and stop him with his arms, while another took a step back and pulled out his gun. Neither man found success. The first one took a bullet from Red's gun right in the face. Blood flew everywhere as the white guard crumpled to the floor. There was a red gash where his face had been.

As the second guard came out with his gun, Red's woman, who was just a step behind him, shot from the hip and took the guard by surprise.

Her first shot hit him high in the chest, spinning him around. The second shot took the back of his head off. The couple ran past, not bothering to see the object of their handiwork fall to the floor.

"Everybody stay still," Kenyatta ordered loudly, "and won't nobody get hurt." As he spoke, a guard on Kenyatta's blind side made his move. As soon as the man reached for his weapon, Betty stepped around her man and raised the sawed-off shotgun she carried in her bag. The gun was cut off so that it was almost as short as a pistol. She gave the man both barrels. The sight of what the shotgun did froze the other men in fear. There was no doubt in their minds now that the blacks meant business.

Kenyatta backed up the ramp, using the girl who had been at the checkpoint as his shield. He stopped and waved Betty and the rest of his crowd past. They rushed up the ramp towards Red, who had the steward shaking from fear under the sight of his gun.

Kenyatta's measured words roared out over the airport. "You honkies had better pay heed, or we'll kill everything white on the plane." A dark flush stained his lean and sallow cheeks as rage glittered in his cold black eyes.

The sight of the terrified white girl in the tall black man's arms made the guards hesitate. There was no doubt that he would kill her. The guards held their weapons in check and allowed Kenyatta to make his way on up the ramp.

Eddie-Bee stood at the top of the ramp waiting for him, while he pointed two thirty-eight short-nosed police specials at the white men at the bottom of the ramp.

"That's right!" Kenyatta roared as he backed into the plane, followed by Eddie-Bee. "If you don't want any dead passengers or stewards, keep your hands off them motherfuckin' guns." His voice carried all the way through the plane, causing a near panic among the passengers.

The members of his gang had already taken complete command of the plane. The pilot of the plane was well aware of the fact that his plane had been commandeered by a bunch of black gunmen. He reached the tower by radio and asked for information on what to do.

"Follow their orders. Don't endanger any of the passengers!" the voice from the tower replied. "The people who have taken control of your plane are murderers. They have just killed at least four people in the terminal, so be careful."

The co-pilot glanced over at the captain; their eyes locked for a quiet moment, but that was broken by the entry of Zeke. The tall black man stood in the cockpit with a cocked gun in his hand. He aimed it at the back of the co-pilot's head. "There won't be any trouble if you don't give us any," the black man stated harshly.

From the way the man spoke, the pilot knew he meant business. "Where to?" the pilot asked softly.

"When we get off the ground, I'll let you know,"

Zeke replied, then smiled. It had gone easier than Kenyatta had said it would. "Wherever we go," he said offhandedly, "you can bet it will be a black country. Yes indeed," Zeke said, speaking more to himself than the white pilots. "It's goin' sure nuff be black!"

Don't miss Mikal Malone's

Pit Bulls in a Skirt 2

Available now from Dafina Books

Prologue

Aleed's black Nike boots pressed against the grungy snow as he ran for his freedom. Having six warrants out for his arrest and a pocket filled with crack rocks, he knew he'd be going down for a long time if the persistent cop caught him.

"Freeze! Stop running before I shoot!" the rookie cop yelled.

The young black cop's loyalty to his job impacted his decisions. All he wanted was Aleed, the man whose picture was pinned against the police station wall, which he saw every day.

"If you don't freeze... I'm gonna fuckin' shoot! I'm not playin' wit you!" the cop taunted. "Stop runnin'!"

When Aleed saw the green awning over the gate in Emerald City, he felt a sense of calm. He *knew that once he got over the gate, the rules the outside world lived by would not apply.*

"This is my final warning," the cop yelled as they ran down the dark sidewalk, a few feet from the level of the fence. Aleed leaped over the fence.

And then the cop heard Aleed yell, "Ecilop! Ecilop!"

The cop thought the yell was weird, but he remained on his trail. He didn't realize that "ecilop" stood for police backward. It was the code word for Emerald City to lock down shop and get out of Dodge.

Instead of hopping the fence like Aleed, the cop ran through the entrance gate, past the empty guard's station, and onto Emerald's grounds. Once inside, he noticed that Emerald appeared vacant. As always, the five buildings of Emerald City encompassed a large yard in the middle. It was pitch dark and no lights were on, not even in the yard. Emerald City was in order.

"Aleed, get out here! Don't make things worse!" The rookie's voice echoed and bounced back to him off the buildings. "Aleed! I know you hear me!"

The gun he was holding shook in his hand, and the darkness and silence frightened him.

Then he heard, "What you doin' here, cop? What you doin' on EC grounds?"

The voice appeared to come from the top of one of the buildings, but the rookie couldn't see the man or his face.

"I'm a police officer, and I'm here for Aleed."

"Well, if you a D.C. cop, you should know your laws don't apply here. Leave now . . . while you still can."

The man's disregard to his shield enraged the rookie cop. "I'm not goin' nowhere without Aleed! I'm the muthafuckin' law!" the officer shouted.

The person laughed, and others laughed behind him; their voices were hidden within the night.

"Check dis out, cop. . . . Right now, the choice is yours to leave. But when I count to three, the choice will be yours no more. We run fuckin' Emerald City and everybody in it!" he yelled at the top of his lungs, sending chills through the cop's tender heart.

"One!" the voice began.

"I'm a police officer!" the rookie yelled, backing up cautiously.

"Two!" was followed by a clicking sound of many weapons upon the rooftops.

"You can't get away with this!" the officer continued.

But before he could say "three," the cop was gone. With his life in tote.

Welcome to Emerald City!

Mercedes

We make this shit look easy.

I can't believe I'm runnin' late! I am dodging in and out of traffic, trying to make it to Emerald City on time. I should not have been fuckin' wit Derrick's sexy ass this morning. That man must've fucked me in every room in our loft-style apartment at D.C.'s National Harbor. Lifting up slightly, I tug at the seat of my Seven jeans between my legs. They were rubbing against my pussy, causing me discomfort, but damn does that boy have some good dick. It's a good thing my kids were with their father, because I'm not sure if I would've been able to keep my voice down.

I thought I knew what love was when I was with Cameron. I couldn't see the Sun or the Moon unless Cameron was with me. It's amazing what separation and a near-death experience can do for a relationship. Bottom line is this, now that I've been in Derrick's presence, I know what real love is; and I'm not willing to trade it for any man in the world . . . not even for Cameron.

When I pull up to the Emerald City gate, I am immediately transformed. No longer am I a girlfriend or a mother. In Emerald City, I'm a boss! Glancing at the five buildings with green awnings circling the open field, I respect its power.

"Good morning, ma'am," says the security guard at the gate. "The other ladies just got here. They're in the field."

"Thanks, Jake. How's the baby?"

"Growing bigger every day." He smiles. "He'll be two tomorrow."

"That's right! It is his birthday."

"Yes, ma'am, it is."

"Well, you can have the day off to spend with your family. I'll get Amir to guard the gate for you."

"Thanks, boss! I appreciate it!"

I wait until the gates open and drive my new black Mercedes-Benz G-Class SUV inside.

Once inside, I see my girls standing outside with their cars surrounding them. It's cold outside, and the sky is icy blue. As usual, they're draped in fur coats and diamonds; I can't help but smile. We were the flyest drug bosses in D.C., hands down! We make this shit look easy. Yvette's red Lincoln Navigator is parked next to Kenyetta's silver Lexus LS; I pull up next to Carissa's blue

Porsche. I can't wait to get out of my ride and hug my friends.

"About time you got here, bitch!" Yvette yells as my girls crowd around.

"Shut your short ass up! Better late than never."

"No . . . your ass always late!" Carissa interjects.

"What is this . . . shorties-gang-up-on-Mercedes day?" I laugh. "Kenyetta, you got my back, right?"

"You know it." She smiles.

We embrace one another. Ever since we made a decision to move out of Emerald and run our operation from the outside, we saw each other less. We talked as much as we could, but we had our own lives. No matter what, we agreed to return and spend a week in Emerald City each month; and no one knew which week we'd choose but us. We did this to remain spontaneous and leave nothing to chance.

I glance at the rooftops and see our shooters in place. Whenever we are in Emerald, security is tighter than security protecting the president.

"Fuck all that bullshit! Look at that truck!" Yvette says. She traded her short, spiky hair for a cute, shoulder-length bob. "When you get that? And what happened to the car?"

"I still got my car. And if you would answer your phone sometimes, you woulda known I got this last Friday," I tell her, examining the black waist-length fur coat she wore with her jeans and black Gucci boots.

"Oh, here we go again," she says, brushing me off. "Like you always answer your phone."

"She's tellin' the truth, Yvette. You ain't the same. Everything good with you?" Carissa questions as she tries to close her full-length chocolate coat tighter. The wind is blowing harder.

"Don't start with me, because we all have personal lives, including me."

"Yvette, we're still family, and family keeps in contact. So you tell us, how are things really going with you?" Kenyetta asks. I notice Yvette's eyes seem sad. "You ain't got no kids or no man—so what's up with you?"

Yvette looks at all of us and drops her head before brushing her hair out of her face. I feel bad for putting her on the spot, but I care about her. I care about all of them. Just because we leave Emerald doesn't mean that changes. We worth fuckin' millions! Niggas would love to kidnap one of us just to make some cash. We have to watch each other's backs.

"What's up, Vette?" I persist.

"Can we just leave it alone, Mercedes? I just need to get into my apartment, grab a drink, and relax. It's cold out here."

"Why you in a rush to go into that lonely-ass apartment, anyway?" Carissa asks, beating her feet for warmth.

"Yeah, bitch!" I tell her, looping my arm through hers. "You do seem a little anxious. You sure you ain't gettin' high on our supply?"

"I'ma fuck you up, Mercedes!" She laughs. "I'ma do better about calling when we away from Emerald. And y'all betta take that because it's all I can give right now. So, can we please get out of this cold air and go inside? Carissa sound like she in a marchin' band or somethin'."

"A'ight, bossy," I tell her. "I'ma let you off the hook for now, but you gonna tell me what's up with you."

"Yeah . . . and if you do have a man, we want to meet him," Carissa adds. "I gotta tell his ass however many times he fuckin' you, he betta increase that shit by three, because you wound up!"

We all laugh.

"Trust me, I'm gettin' sexed more than all of y'all put together. I guarantee that."

"Doubt it!" I laugh.

"That's real talk! Way more!"

"Oh . . . really," Kenyetta says. "I guess we better get inside our apartments, drop our shit off, and finish this meeting so we can hear the juicy details."

We chitchat a little longer and jump in our rides. As I pull off, I can't help but think about Yvette again. Something is definitely up.

Don't miss Reign's

Hate List 2

Available now from Dafina Books!

Prologue

Yvonna looked at her nude body in the full-length mirror on the bathroom door. She examined herself, as she had many times before.

"Who am I?"

That question wasn't about the curves in her hips or how her breasts were still as perky as they were months after cosmetic surgery. The question was about her mental stability and why it always seemed that everyone she loved—for one reason or another—could never love her back.

She turned around and, through the open doorway, stared at Dave's body on the bed. A single tear fell down her face as she realized a love lost. The glossy blood from his throat dripped out of his body and fell against the wooden floor.

She loved him with the kind of love she had as

a child, when she played with a brand-new doll on Christmas Day. This was before her father had raped her, stealing any innocence or understanding she had of life. All she wanted was love. Yet, a part of her—the part she called Gabriella—loved nothing more than to cause destruction to those who crossed her path. Gabriella was how she protected her feelings.

As the steam from the running shower filled the bathroom and covered the mirror, she smoothed it off with her left hand. Another tear fell down her cheek as she readied herself for what she was about to do. Kill again. Feeling extreme contempt caused Gabriella to appear behind her wearing a one-piece tight red dress.

She placed a hand on her shoulder and whispered in her ear: "Think of it this way. Once they're gone, you'll be happy. Isn't that what you want?"

"Yes." She nodded.

"Good." Gabriella kissed her cheek. She looked just like Taraji P. Henson from the movie Baby Boy. *"Now do it. Get mad. And get even. Let's finish what you started."*

Yvonna wiped the onerous tear off her face and grabbed the knife off the edge of the white porcelain sink.

With revenge and malice overflowing, she carved into the flesh of her right shoulder the names of the people she hated most. Although the blade tore through her soft skin, she didn't flinch.

The pain was pleasurable as she watched the names of the people she despised appear with oozing blood. When she was done, she wiped the red fluid off her skin with her free hand and smiled:

Bernice
Cream
Jhane
Swoopes

Yvonna was beyond crazy.
Yvonna was beyond mad.
Hate consumed her so much that it was difficult to breathe at times. And with Gabriella being unleashed, it was impossible for her to be controlled.

Catch a Co-Conspirator
by Her Toe

Yvonna and Gabriella stand quietly backstage as they watch the middle-school children act out a scene from a play the students wrote called *A Midwinter Night Scream*. Colorful costumes dress the floor, empty chairs, and equipment as they run from the stage to the back to prepare for each scene.

Like snakes waiting to attack, they remain still. Their eyes are fixated on two children—and nothing or nobody would stand in their way. They have to get them.

"Hi, I'm Mrs. Princely. Can I help you?" asks a beautiful black woman with soft, curly, shoulder-length hair. Her face is stern when she approaches Yvonna from behind.

"No, I'm just watching my niece. Isn't she beautiful?" Yvonna looks at the stage, at no child in particular.

The woman's face softens immediately. After all, Yvonna looks nothing like the average abductor. In fact, she looks stylish in her dark blue custom-made jeans and red leather jacket. Her hair is styled in her trademark short, spiky cut. Just the way she likes it.

"Oh . . . which one is yours?" The teacher smiles, looking upon the stage with Yvonna as the children sing a wretched ballad.

Yvonna doesn't have an answer for the nosy bitch and she wishes she would just leave her the fuck alone. She doesn't, though.

"Tell the bitch her name is Lil Reecy or some shit!" Gabriella yells from the sidelines. She is wearing an all-red leather jumper by Baby Phat. "Make somethin' up! Think on your feet! Haven't I taught you anything?"

"Be quiet! You makin' a scene, and shit!" Yvonna tells her.

"Are you okay?" the woman asks.

"Oh . . . uh . . . yeah."

She scrutinizes her. "Well . . . who are you talking to?"

"No one. Just had an outburst. That's it."

Yvonna has worked so hard to control Gabriella, but nothing succeeds. She is still convinced that Gabriella is real; it's just that other people can't see her.

"If you say so. Well, which one is your niece?"

Yvonna scans the crowd of brats and picks the homeliest-looking one she can find. If truth be told, not a one of them looks like she's seen any parts of a tub, soap, or water—ever.

"That one right there." She points at a girl with pink barrettes in her hair and a bright yellow sunshine costume. "She's my niece."

"Who? Tabitha?"

Yvonna can tell by the woman's expression that she could not imagine a child so afflicted being related to her in any form or fashion.

"You just had to pick 'Snot-Nosed-Nancy,' didn't you?" Gabriella laughs. "Don't be surprised if she don't believe you now."

Yvonna ignores her and says, "Yes. She's my niece. I just got back in town and wanted to surprise her. So when I found out at the last minute about the play, I ran over here. I wanted to be the first person she hugs when she steps off the stage."

"Wow! Oh . . . uh . . . I can't wait to see the look on her face!" The woman beams. "No one ever supports her in school. Not to say anything bad about your family."

"No worries," Yvonna reassures her, touching the teacher lightly on the arm. "My sister's a hot-ass mess, I know it."

The woman gasps. Yvonna ignores her reaction.

"But you should get on out of my face." Yvonna stops and clears her throat and says, "I mean, you should go back out there. The kids need you."

"They're fine. I want to be here to see Tabitha's face when she sees you."

This woman is causing Yvonna's blood to boil. If this bitch knows what's good for her, she'll get lost before she shows up missing . . . permanently. Because nothing or nobody would stop Yvonna from snatching Treyana's kids; and she would not mind covering her tracks and witnesses if they got in her way. She never thought deceiving Treyana's sons into leaving out the back door with her would be so difficult.

"Hurry up and get rid of her! They almost done!" Gabriella yells.

Gabriella is growing agitated, so Yvonna has to think quickly. Her mind wanders and she grapples with choking the fuck out of the old-ass crow or smacking her down. She decides upon smacking her, until she sees a little girl holding her hands between her legs, running toward the restroom. The glittery purple shoes she wears causes a devilish idea to enter her mind.

"Excuse me," Yvonna says to the woman. "I have to go to the restroom before my niece comes out."

"No problem! I'll be waiting right here when you get back. I can't wait to see the look on her face!"

Man, this whore is about to make me unleash! Why she gotta be all in my fuckin' business?

Yvonna makes her way past the children who are roaming around backstage. She sees a small bucket on the floor filled with costume jewelry for the performance. She takes one look behind her to see if the woman is watching—she isn't. A little girl who needs help changing a costume has taken her attention.

So Yvonna dips inside the restroom and looks under the stalls until she sees the purple shoes the little girl is wearing. When she spots them, she goes into the stall next to her and dumps the jewelry on the floor. Afterward, she uses the bucket to scoop out some water from the commode. There is shit and piss inside, but Yvonna doesn't care. She stands up on the commode and dumps the foul feces all over the little girl, who screams in terror.

Yvonna's laughter prohibits her from running as fast as she wants to while exiting the bathroom. She manages to calm herself down moments before approaching the woman.

"I think something's wrong with one of the children in the restroom. I saw another little girl playing an awful joke on her. Hurry!" Yvonna appears frantic. "Go help her! Please!"

The woman drops the clipboard she's holding and runs toward the bathroom. When she leaves, Yvonna regains her focus as she watches Treyana's kids come backstage after their roles. She's amazed at how cute they are—with their fluffy, curly hair and wide-eyed smiles—despite the costumes they are wearing that make them look like two fruity bitches. In her opinion they didn't look like Treyana or her husband.

"You boys were wonderful!" Yvonna cheers. "I'm so proud of you."

"Who are you?" one of the twins asks. "You look familiar."

Yvonna has been around them, but not often, and she is surprised they remember. One of them is slightly taller than the other, but they are otherwise identical.

"I'm your aunt Paris! You don't remember me?" Yvonna touches her heart and appears hurt.

"No," the other one responds. "I never heard of you."

"That's awful! You really haven't heard of your aunt Paris from Texas?"

The twins look at each other again and shake their heads no.

"Don't worry about that right now. We'll have plenty of time for catch up." She smiles. "But right now, I need you to come with me. Your mom wants me to take you home. We'll talk about everything on the way there."

"But Momma said never to leave with a stranger," one of them says.

"A stranger?" Yvonna folds her arms and stands on her back foot. "I doubt very seriously that a stranger would be dressed as good as I am. Now, are you coming or not? It don't make me no never mind," Yvonna lies.

Whether the boys know it or not, they are leaving that school with her—even if she has to snatch them by their undeveloped balls.

They look at each other and then at her. She
knows they're examining her stylish shoes and
her pretty face. She smiles. She doesn't look harm-
ful, and she does everything she can to conceal
her pleasure. Men always become her victims.

*Little do you know, but the Devil has many
faces*, she silently says.

The taller one shrugs his shoulders, looks at
the shorter one, and replies, "Okay. Let's go."

"Great! And I brought some candy for you too.
I figured you'd like it."

Like all kids experience, when they come into
contact with sweet poison . . . it is lust at first sight.